the SUMMER of the
DISCO KING

JANE HARVEY MEADE

*To Sally,
Wishing you
luck with your
own writing
career. Keep in
touch.
Love,
Jane*

SUMMER OF THE DISCO KING
©2011 Jane Harvey Meade

Txu 1-757-045
May 23, 2011

ISBN: 978-1-936447-58-9

All rights reserved. No part of this book may be reproduced in any form or by any electronic or mechanical means, including information storage and retrieval systems, without permission in writing from the author, except by a reviewer, who may quote brief passages in review.

This is a work of fiction. Names, characters, places, and incidents either are the product of the author's imagination or are used fictitiously, and any resemblance to actual persons, living or dead, is coincidental.

Designed and Printed by
Maine Authors Publishing
558 Main Street, Rockland, Maine 04841
www.maineauthorspublishing.com

ACKNOWLEDGEMENTS

My thanks to Genie Dailey of Custom Museum Publishing, Inc., and Maine Authors Publishing for her scrupulous editing. My thanks, as well, to Cheryl McKeary of the above company for fielding all of my many questions about the fine art of getting my book into print.

Thanks to my readers who helped to give me moral support and valuable suggestions:
Evora Bunker Mattson of Bucksport, Maine
Cousin Susan Haggerty of Winterport, Maine
Cousin Judith Mountain of Dexter, Maine

Thank you, Lisa Marie Parker, my daughter, for encouraging me to make *Summer of the Disco King* my first published novel.

And thank you to my "like a daughter," Tina Simonelli for her always at my call help with this computer machine.

And to my brother, Dr. Peter Harvey of Hartford, Connecticut, who edited all of my writing with his usual wit and humor before his untimely death in 2005. I miss you every day.

the SUMMER of the
DISCO KING

a novel

CHAPTER 1

I was tired of living alone. My teenage daughter and I had been rattling around in our four-bedroom Colonial for over three years, ever since my husband had died, and the painful echoes of the place, though subdued, were still audible. It was time to have a boarder, really, I kept telling myself that morning as I sat on the front steps waiting for Franny.

It was the first day of summer vacation, and to this teacher's mind, the best day of the year. Equivalent in expectancy to dozens of Christmas Eves. On the first day of summer vacation, I anticipated two months and ten days of Christmases loaded with toys to my liking—hot, lazy, free days full of peace and quiet and endeavors which I wished to do. No schedules; no five-thirty alarm clocks ringing.

Still, I had gotten up early this first day just the same. I'd walked my six miles and was enjoying my first cup of coffee at only seven-fifteen. The whole day ahead! The whole summer ahead! My good mood assured me that Franny was just the ticket to take the edge off the empty feeling the house still gave me and the answer for my lack of companionship (especially when my fifteen-year-old could only reply, "Oh, Mom, that's dumb" or "Oh, Mom, that's gross" or "Oh, Mom, that's sick"). Besides, the heating bills had been astronomical this past winter, and I could use the extra income that renting a room would provide.

On top of this, it was Franny, not a stranger, coming to live here. Though not close friends, we had known each other through our husbands for twenty years, and even after she and her husband divorced, she'd come around at least once a year, bringing her good nature and overactive enthusiasm for life, not to mention her fertile imagination, with her. She and I would chat on and on about all her occult and UFO experiences since we'd seen each other last, and I'd find myself telling her things I'd never share with anyone else for fear they'd think I was crazy.

Franny was sure she was a very old soul dating back at least to the beginning of Egyptian history. A fortune teller had told her that once, verifying what Franny had suspected all along.

For someone who craved good conversation, I certainly had the most provocative conversationalist I could ever hope for in Franny. That was why I had immediately agreed to rent her a room when she had to temporarily move out of an apartment she was renovating.

So why this feeling of apprehension?

Franny's zest for life included a great appetite for men. All kinds of men. All colors, ages, and creeds of men, and a few women, she'd confessed to me during one of our yearly conversations. I'd tried to nod nonchalantly so she wouldn't think my gaping mouth meant a negative judgment on my part. If I enjoyed Franny's eccentricities, I had to learn to look the other way with some of them, I supposed.

I had managed to lay down a few basic rules of the "no visitors past the first floor" variety without hurting her feelings. She had been the one, in fact, to cite the tender and budding attitudes of my daughter, which must, she insisted, be protected at all costs. She did this in the warm, sincere manner which was so typically Franny, thus sparing me from a litany of excuses or apologies for my own embarrassingly tender naiveté. I was forty—too old and too honest not to recognize my own squareness in these circular '80s.

As I sat engrossed in my thoughts of stunted attitudes, the Disco King rode by, top down on his ugly, paint-stripped, now-purple '69 Chrysler convertible, radio blasting as usual.

"Mom," a voice called from an upstairs window when the car had taken a turn at the corner, and the music was only partially audible from at least two blocks over, "that was the Disco King."

"I know," I hollered up to the voice, "you've already pointed him out twice before. What's his real name?" I had a theory that whenever teenagers cared enough to share information with you, you had best show some interest or it might be a long time before they confided in you again.

"Who knows?" came the reply, with a heavy accent on the *knows* and a tone that said "Who cares?" with much clarity.

"Dumb question," I muttered into my cup as I took a sip of coffee. I figured it would be a few weeks anyway before she told me anything else.

More cars were beginning to pass by on their way to work. The Disco King had been out early. I thought of hollering a second question to the voice at the window with regard to where a young man such as the Disco King might be headed at this early hour of the morning, but remembering the scorn concerning my first question, I thought better of it.

"Who cares?" I echoed into my cup.

I loved this house, this street, my home for six years now. Spanning the entire block opposite my white-and-brick Colonial was a housing complex for the elderly. It fronted four streets in its swing around one city block. It was a modern, two-story brick compound with white pillars supporting terraced balconies. A crew of gardeners and handymen groomed and landscaped it daily, thus preserving its new appearance at all times. Over the last two years, I had gotten into the routine of walking the circumference of the complex twelve times a day, a calculated distance of six miles. I had become addicted to the habit, addicted to the feeling of stronger and stronger legs propelling my body, which had melted into a lean, firm frame. I had proudly built up to the rate of six miles an hour. Fellow teachers who were seasoned joggers could only average seven or eight miles an hour. Of course, they went farther than six miles a day, but the books said that rate and distance were not important; rather the time spent in the movement was the key.

When I told people of my custom of circling the same block a dozen times a day, they looked incredulous. Didn't I feel like a fool? Didn't I get bored on the same constant route? I told them that, at forty, I'd earned the right to do whatever I pleased, foolish or not, and that there was no boredom in walking. It was not the scenery which titillated the spirit; it was the exercise itself.

The familiar and glistening maroon Cadillac cruised by. Happy, behind the wheel, slowly touched the brim of his summer straw hat and nodded at me with raised eyebrows and a half-smile, almost in the manner of someone in a grand parade, someone of royalty whose subjects are lined up along his way. I responded with an energetic wave. I loved Happy. It had nothing to with with the fact that he had been an immeasurable help in procuring this house. He had been kind to us, it was true, but he was an irresistible seventy-year- old character who felt like forty and thought like twenty and embraced every moment of life with an exuberance that put him on a special plane in my judgment.

"Hey, Kiddo!" he'd shout to me on his daily jog by the house. I'd look up from my weeding and sit back on my heels to study his sturdy old legs as they carried him at respectable speed up and around the corner. It always made me wonder about the durability of my own hot and tired forty-year-old body as I wiped the sweat from my forehead and guiltily went back to pulling weeds with what I hoped was a vigor befitting my age.

Why Happy called me Kiddo, I had no idea, unless he just didn't remember my name, which I found a reasonable explanation. First, he had dealt mainly with my husband in the transfer of this property, which had belonged to his son and daughter-in-law. Secondly, I had gotten the distinct impression that almost his sole concern in those days was finalizing the sale so that they would be free to leave the area as soon as possible.

He had confided to my husband that his life would become infinitely more peaceful when they had removed themselves from the East Coast and taken all their problems with them to a new home in California. I had felt badly that Happy had had to be troubled with grown children who were my own age, and surely old enough to take care of their own lives by this time, especially since Happy also had an invalid and often weak-minded wife to worry about. One hardly ever saw her except on rare summer days when she felt well enough to stroll in her robe and hairnet along the sidewalk outside my door.

I had invited Sarah in on such occasions. I knew she missed her son and longed to touch him in some way, perhaps by pausing and staring at this house that had once welcomed her as the paternal grandmother. The tears that would well up in her eyes as she stood gazing at my home would be dispelled when I escorted her inside. She'd sit quietly on the sofa in the living room, cooled and darkened by thick window shades pulled against the afternoon heat of July or August. What talk there was would be gnarled like her hands by an obviously confused mind. Whatever thoughts haunted her on these visits seemed to rejuvenate Sarah, for upon leaving, her movements seemed less stiff and her face more serene.

I watched a bird draw a long brown worm from a patch of grass next to the hedges. It was a good sign, the worm. It meant the soil was getting rich. Maybe the grass would be thicker this year. Every spring since I'd lived here, I'd fussed over the dry, yellowed lawn until at least some areas showed young patches of pastel green from the new seeds and fertilizer I'd sprinkled about. Now I sipped at my coffee and stared at the grass as if the secret of having a beautiful lawn like the Peddingtons' on the next block was written in the lines of the cracked soil around the balding green patches of grass.

"Hey, Kiddo!" A voice flew by above feet that slapped at the sidewalk in front of me. "All done with school, huh?" he threw back over his shoulder.

"You bet," I laughed after his fleeting back.

"Mom, if anyone calls, I'm not here."

"You going somewhere?" I looked up at the teenager who had come out onto the steps and made the announcement with a heavy sigh.

"No, Mom," came the impatient retort as if I should have known better than to ask such a question. "Where would I go at this hour of the morning? It's only eight o'clock. I just don't want to waste such a beautiful part of the day on the telephone."

"I'm surprised you're even up, first day off."

"Well, no sense lying around. I might as well get up and enjoy my vacation." Another heavy sigh punctuated this mature observation.

"My thoughts exactly."

When there was no further dialogue, I turned to look behind me. No one was there. My daughter had evidently melted into thin air, a magical trick she had suddenly been able to do ever since entering eighth grade.

I sipped the last dregs from my cup and decided that this brief conversation, like all my conversations with Jana lately, had been going downhill before it had even begun, and her disappearing act served to preserve at least a modicum of civility between us. I endeavored to concentrate on being thankful for my daughter's Houdini-like talents

It was then, as I attempted this reflection and started to get up from the steps to refill my cup, that Franny's tiny foreign car pulled up. She waved glibly, threw open the driver's door, and with surprising agility wrenched her rotund frame from where it had been wedged behind the wheel.

Bouncing after her was a small white terrier.

"Who's that?" I asked, dreading the answer.

"Oh, didn't I tell you about Terrance?"

She had let the dog go loose, and he was going all right, "going" right in the middle of the only 3' by 5' section of lawn that had managed to achieve a pastel green!

"No," I replied weakly, "you left that part out."

"Well," Franny spoke into the trunk as she started dragging out suitcases and boxes, "he's a real love and completely housebroken."

"I can tell," I grumbled as I looked for a shovel under the steps.

"Jana," I yelled for my daughter, "come help Franny with her things!"

I found the shovel.

"Jana!" I tried again as I crossed the front walk.

When I reached the soiled spot and began scooping deposits onto the tip of the spade, it dawned on me that my daughter's disappearing act had lasted longer than usual. I wondered briefly if she'd gone back to bed after all.

"Jana!" I yelled up to the screened windows of the second

floor.

A moment later, a face appeared at one of the screens. "Mom," came a voice full of carefully controlled impatience, "please, give me a break! I'm talking on the phone."

I stood momentarily dazed as I posed against the shovel like a cowhand. Hadn't it been only a few minutes ago that my daughter had professed her reluctance to talk to anyone on the phone, or was I losing my mind?

As if in answer to my question, I watched Franny make the first pass through the front door with a box and a suitcase, as Terrance made a second pass at the young maple tree on my side lawn.

CHAPTER 2

The sun was over Martha's house next door, an orange globe in the late afternoon sky. During the day it had passed around my Colonial and would now set, with its glowing promise of another hot day tomorrow, in front of my maple tree. I was sitting at the umbrella table by the pool on the top deck at the back of the house and absently swirling the lime around in a Dubonnet. My thoughts were about what I had not accomplished on my first full day of vacation. So I endeavored to map out, in my mind, the chores I would tackle tomorrow.

But out on the deck this afternoon, I'd also had time to reconsider my decision to have Franny move in with us. Unfortunately, this came one day too late. By five o'clock, she was half unpacked and taking her accustomed nap before work, sleeping like a baby even on her first day in a new place, and signaling how oblivious she could be to catastrophe even with all her ESP, auras, and incantations. I made a mental note to ask her how many lives a soul needed to live before it could innately sense disaster.

Terrance, disaster number one, was tied in the dog run that had been built by the first owner and (up to now) unused by the second owner. I imagined him depositing about a quarter pound an hour, which would have to be constantly removed (God knew how, by whom, and to where) if we didn't want to be assailed by the pungent aromas of dog poop, as my daughter would have delicately phrased it, during our swimming and sunbathing activities of a hot afternoon.

With that thought, I moved to the lower deck, the one furthest removed from Terrance. From this vantage point, the only hint of his existence was the occasional sound of a chain dragged over cement, reminding me of Marley in my favorite Christmas story, which I determined never to read again.

The decks in the backyard were laid out in bright yellows and oranges and tied together with deep chocolate-brown floor edgings and rails. My husband had built and decorated them, carpeting the lower deck in an orange tweed with rose and yellow in the weave. Steps led to a second deck that completely circled an above-ground pool. This upper deck was carpeted by striped Astroturf of bright orange and black. Around the base of the decks were skirts of orange canvas anchored and kept taut by a board stapled neatly along the bottom. I marveled at the durability of his creation, and wondered how long it would last in the wake of Terrance.

Franny was already dropping hints about how a dog needed his freedom to run as she looked over our completely fenced-in backyard. And every time my eye fell on the gate by the side of the house next to the dog run, I was tempted to let Terrance have *complete* freedom.

I sipped my Dubonnet on the rocks at my orange-covered picnic table (I was the genius who had taken an old orange plastic window shade and stapled it to the top of the table), and I considered how desperate Franny might become if Terrance disappeared tonight for good.

Just above me, Franny's window curtains slapped every so often against the screen. I had given her the Blue Room, an empty guest room that no one had used since we'd owned the house.

Over the fence to my right and across the court, I watched Martha come out of her door and sway precariously as she carefully planted first one, then the other foot on each of the three wooden steps down to her side lawn. It was after five. She'd had her supper and now carried the scraps of it on a plate for the local birds' nightly repast. Beneath her umbrella-shaped clothesline, she scattered the crumbs. If she saw me, she didn't acknowledge it. For some reason, we didn't communicate when I was on my back decks, but only when I was in the front yard, which directly paralleled her side entrance. Then she would patter in her slippers across the narrow court street to gossip with me about the goings-on of the neighbors with her crisp German accent and equally crisp and clear eighty-five-year-old wit. She was the landlady and owner of the first house on the street, but she lived alone. I watched out for her. Sort of. She was feisty, but vulnerable.

Just last month, she'd had a terrible scare. She had left for a minute to carry some chicken soup to a friend in the old-age complex. As she related the story to me later, she had left the door unlocked as usual, since she never left her home for more than five minutes. But she was gone long enough that time for a man to wander in. He was perched on her kitchen table when she returned. Taken aback, she reversed direction momentarily with her hand over her heart, gasping that he had scared her out of her wits. He looked at her, now paralyzed, and she back at him. They stared at each other in this way for several life-draining seconds, until, brushing by her without a word, he exited the way he'd come in.

It had been her deduction, and subsequently mine, that he had been spaced-out on drugs. From then on, Martha had not neglected to keep her doors locked day and night, home or not. I had always been paranoid about such things anyway, but I must confess that I was even more so after hearing of Martha's experience.

"To my first day of vacation," I mused, lifting my Dubonnet in mock toast to the summer in an effort to cast away thoughts of what could have happened to Martha. Usually, half of an ice-filled glass of Dubonnet was enough to make me terribly drowsy, viciously hungry, or inexcusably drunk. This afternoon, warm as it was, the sweet red wine managed to be impotent to my tenuous chemistry.

Music, disco music, sailed across the row of backyards to my left and invaded my reverie. Had I been in blissful repose, I might have resented the intrusion. As it was, I didn't bat an eye. Happy's grandson, who had stayed behind when his parents had left this house and the East Coast, was playing his stereo again.

"Happy's grandson is playing his stereo," my daughter announced unnecessarily as she appeared at the sliding porch screen.

"Yes, I noticed," I nodded and motioned to her. "Come out here a minute."

"What!" It was not a question. I bit my lip as she slapped the screen door open and stepped out onto the deck.

"Please close the screen," I coaxed, trying to sound friendly.

"What!" came that snappy voice full of impatience again and accompanied this time by a hand on one hip.

"Where are you going?" I asked, suddenly noticing the freshly shampooed hair and the scent of Charlie cologne.

"Nowhere," came the same irritated tone.

"Well, you look so dressed up. You really look nice. I like the shirt." I looked closer. "In fact," I sat forward abruptly for a clearer look, "I like the shirt so much, I bought it last week."

A slight smile curved ever so reluctantly across my daughter's face.

"That's my shirt, isn't it?" I asked.

No reply. Just the smile. If it weren't for the fact that my daughter hadn't smiled at me since eighth grade, I'd have lost my temper and demanded she remove the blouse that I hadn't even worn yet.

"Mom, I just had to wear something that would match my Sassons."

I looked closer still. "*My* Sassons," I corrected. I'd bought them last month. I'd worn them twice. "Where are you going that's so important?" I persisted.

"I promised Franny I'd feed the dog," was the answer.

"And for this you need my new shirt? Not to mention my 'old' Sassons?"

Jana didn't answer, but with what was supposed to be a disgusted shake of her head, walked down the steps to the black-topped floor under and around the decks on her way to the dog run.

A strange, shrill and screeching wail from the front street commanded my attention, and I looked to see a big produce truck pull around Grayson Street and pass my house. It gave its strange and grating call once more before it left my sight.

"What was that?" Jana asked, now at the other side of the backyard with the dog, which was running back and forth in its excitement at having some company.

"A fruit and vegetable truck," I answered. "Never saw it before."

"It blotted out the best part of 'Boogie-Oogie-Oogie' by Taste of Honey that Percy was playing," she said in disgust, and I realized that everything my adolescent daughter said to me was in disgust.

"What was that?" a disheveled Franny appeared above me at the screened window, and I almost jumped. For a second, I had forgotten there were more than just Jana and me on the premises.

"Happy's grandson, Percy, plays his stereo a bit loudly at times," I answered.

"I mean, what screamed like that? It blocked out the best part of 'Boogie- Oogie-Oogie,'" Franny complained.

"Oh, a vegetable and fruit truck. It's a new one on me," I shrugged, quickly calculating the difference in age between my daughter and Franny, who had come up with the same reaction. I stored the useless thought for future reference in case I ever needed to use it in a discussion about choices Franny was making and her maturity level—a discussion I felt was imminent every time I looked at the wretched dog she'd "forgotten" to tell me about.

"What are you drinking?" Franny's eyes lighted on my tall, hourglass- shaped goblet full of ice and half-full of Dubonnet.

"Want one?" I asked, suddenly liking the feeling of comradeship that had been lacking since Joe died. You couldn't very well share a Dubonnet with a sophomore, not to mention a pleasant conversation.

"I'll be right down," she said, disappearing from the window.

I went in and found another goblet that matched mine, filled it with ice, and let the red elixir of Dubonnet flow slowly over the cubes. I handed the tempting product to Franny as she entered the kitchen.

Her hair was standing up on her head and lying flat by her ears. The false eyelash that had, at one time, adhered to her left lid, was now glued to her cheekbone.

"My God, Franny," I gasped, "you're a mess."

"I don't need much sleep," she answered, sipping the drink I had handed her, "but what time I do sleep, I sleep deeply. You see the result."

"I'm glad you don't need much sleep," I said, "because with that kind of devastation, I shudder to think what havoc would be wrought in a normal eight hours."

"What is this?" Franny asked, taking another exploratory sip. "I'm a bartender and this is nothing I've ever tried before. It's scrumptious."

"You've never tried *ze* Dubonnet on *ze* ice, then," I said, feigning a French accent. "Does *zis* mean you *haf* never incarnated into *ze* French lineage?

"*Contraire, contraire,*" Franny matched my bad French with her own. "I *vas* Marie Antoinette's dress designer, Yvonne Duprey."

"I detect from your pronunciation of *vas* that you were Eva Braun's dressmaker, as well," I laughed.

Franny was laughing right along with me when she stopped suddenly. "Are you drunk?" she asked, raising her meticulously plucked eyebrows.

"I can get that way on this stuff," I agreed in my own American tongue. "With Terrance and all the excitement, I didn't think I was affected at all."

"You're affected," Franny decided as she moved through the dining room and toward the sliding doors by the deck.

"Well," I said, following her, "I don't deny that this stuff goes right to where you live."

I guess I giggled a bit when I said that because Franny paused to regard me in mid-step onto the deck.

"Do you drink like this every day?"

"Only my first day of summer vacation when it comes on the same day that I adopt a dog," I replied glibly.

"You think you've got problems! I don't know when I'll ever unpack," she said in good-natured frustration, and she and I, with tinkling glasses in hand, settled ourselves into deck chairs. "I just spent six restless hours dozing off and on between twelve boxes, a stereo console practically on my feet, and a dozen stuffed animals in assorted positions around my head. That makes for some strange dreams. Talk about strange bedfellows. . ." Franny sipped her drink. I could tell she was carefully considering something.

"I've had stranger bedfellows, come to think about it," she chuckled, evidently at some private memories that had been resurrected.

I had just started to take a final swallow from my first glass of Dubonnet, part of which ended in a spurt that fortunately went back into the glass.

"You're a nut, Franny," I managed to say. "The only thing that's unfunny about you is your damn dog."

"Terrance? He's a love," Franny avowed for the umpteenth time.

"He's white, you know," I said, wiggling the bit of ice I had left in the glass and sipping the final dregs.

"Are all teachers as quick at picking up details as you are?" Franny asked snidely.

"Well, my entire brown shag carpeting and every stick of furniture has been able to pick up white dog hair in the brief eight hours he's been here. Another day and the décor will be Blizzard of '78."

"Oh, I forgot to tell you that about Terrance."

"You forgot to tell me about Terrance, period."

"I'll feed him some olive oil in his food and that will stop a lot of the shedding."

"Why don't you do the humane thing for me and Terrance and feed him poison? That would stop the shedding entirely. At least then he'd only shed in the spot he dropped dead in. I could live with that."

"You could, but Terrance couldn't. Wait and see if you don't just love him in another week."

I mumbled something about dog abuse into my empty glass and started to get up for a refill.

"Isn't that your third fill-up?" Franny eyed me suspiciously. Then, glancing at her watch, she jumped up from the chair with surprising fluidity of motion for someone of her size. "Lord! If I get to the restaurant late for the tenth night in a row, my boss will absolutely kill me. Now, you don't have to let Terrance out once you let him in. I'll do that when I get home at one or thereabouts. As hostess, I can leave with the last customer most nights."

I looked at my empty wine glass and decided that it was too small to hold an adequate amount of beverage at any one time. Franny followed me through the sliding doors, continuing to jabber about feeding Terrance for the evening and seemingly oblivious to my frantic search through kitchen cupboards for a bigger goblet. She left me on my hands and knees getting reacquainted with a low back shelf I had not seen in several years. I could hear Franny in her bathroom at the top of the stairs as I reluctantly refilled the original glass, having decided with disappointment that that was as big a glass as I was going to find.

Once back outside, my head began to feel like lead. Maybe Franny had been right about this being my third and not my second drink. Whatever, leaden was not the feeling I wanted in late afternoon, so I set the glass on the picnic table and strolled mindlessly to the top deck. At the edge of the pool, I checked the color of the water. It was clear but would need chlorine before morning. I doubted if Jana would be swimming tonight, remembering her freshly done hairdo, and I knew I wouldn't be swimming unless I had suicidal tendencies, what with my two (or three) Dubonnets. Terrance hadn't driven me to any thoughts of self-destruction yet, so I added half a cup of chlorine.

Jana's voice drifted across the back court. She was laughing with her girlfriend Laurie outside Laurie's home, which was directly in back of ours on the other side of a fence and a narrow street.

The screen door of the green house between Martha's and Laurie's banged, and I looked up in time to see my neighbor stride across the front porch and down the steps to his car. He was obviously fresh out of the shower; a crisply pressed short-sleeved shirt lay open at his neck, and he was tucked into a pair of light tan pants with a crease you could cut your finger on. I could almost smell the aftershave from where I stood, and I knew that he had applied the final pat of the lotion to the dark hairs exposed by the shirt's vee. I knew this the way I knew he was a virile, often thoroughly exasperating macho type with enough chemistry to zap me across a court, a fence, and a swimming pool. If I made a habit of watching Martha, I made a *career* out of watching this guy. One of these days I'd learn something more substantial about him, like what he did for a living, or even his name.

Now I made a pretense of tossing chlorine powder across the pool's surface long after every particle had been eliminated from the measuring cup while I watched him back his Mustang out of the driveway. It was after six. He'd be on his way to his girlfriend's, probably going out to dinner. She was blonde but rather dowdy-looking, I thought. He'd brought her to his house several times. Last year he'd had a brunette. She hadn't been much to write home about either. So much for sour grapes.

I replaced the cup in the tub, sealed it shut, and went to get my Dubonnet on the picnic table. I had no sooner lifted the glass to my lips when my friend Dale drove up and parked by the fence.

"If I wasn't on duty, I'd join you," he grinned, leaning across the seat of the cruiser.

I gave him a slow nod, pursing my lips and trying to stifle a callous comeback. "Let me guess," I said finally, putting my free hand to my forehead in the manner of a soothsayer, "you've left Cindy. For the eighth time. This week."

"We had a bad one," the grin belonged to a chastised little boy. It spread candidly beneath large soulful eyes and a head full of dark curls.

"Aren't they all!" I responded, continuing to mock him and ignoring any inclination I might have had to give him a big hug and an "it will get better" kiss.

"Would you keep a lonely, upset guy company at dinner tomorrow night?" The eyebrows rose plaintively.

"You know I won't," I said with a scowl that was my best school-teacher- is-critical look.

"Coffee and Danish? I'll pick you up for breakfast. I'd like to talk to you. To someone with a brain and sensitivity."

"No, Dale. We've been all over this before. I can't get in the middle."

"If I wasn't so damned charming, you'd go out with me," he was grinning mischievously again.

"That's it," I laughed, "you're too charming for your own good."

"I'll be in touch," were his final words, spoken seriously with sober eye contact before he squared himself up behind the wheel again.

I stood and watched him drive off. When he got to the end of the court, he must have gotten a call because his blue lights began to flash and then his siren screamed. I listened to it grow weaker and weaker in the distance until I could no longer hear it at all.

I took a second sip of my drink, which was growing very old and watery. Because of the lapse of so much time between sips, I had begun to feel mostly normal again.

"Do I have my keys? Yes, here they are." Franny, wigged, eyelashed, painted to perfection, and wrapped in a multicolored silky frock that flowed gently around her full figure, stood in an aura of Chanel No. 5 as she groped through her purse and then stared at the keys she'd just retrieved from it. Franny was beautiful, with a face that closely resembled Elizabeth Taylor's, and her perfect taste in wardrobe selections and makeup application neutralized any flaws.

"What is that? Another drink?" she looked at me a bit squinty-eyed.

"Same one," I saluted her with it and took another sip. "I had a couple of interruptions."

"I noticed," Franny looked off to where the cruiser had disappeared. "I didn't know you knew Dale Mercer. How long has this been going on?"

"First of all, nothing is going on," I countered firmly.

"There isn't a girl in town can resist him. Are you telling me you can?"

"He and his wife were friends of Joe's and mine. They both still are." I accentuated the word *both*.

"I hear they don't get along worth a damn."

"They have their troubles," I had to agree, "but he takes everything that happens on the job personally, and that tends to shatter his nerves and make him difficult to live with."

"Well, I would love the opportunity to soothe his nerves." Franny looked at her watch. "You will bring Terrance in, won't you?" she said as she turned to leave.

"I suppose so," I muttered, taking another sip of my drink and sitting down on the deck bench.

"Mummy will be back tonight!" she yelled to Terrance when she got to the screen door. "We'll have a nice walk then, and I'll give you a treat."

I could hear the chain thrashing violently at the sound of Franny's voice. I just swigged my Dubonnet and kept my mouth shut about what kind of nice walk it would be at one o'clock in the morning with an ignorant dog on the other end of the leash.

Just as Franny was pulling away, the phone rang. By the time I reached it, it had rung eight times, which indicated how fast I was moving after my wines. I knew it had to be Joey. Anyone else would have hung up by this time except dependable friend Joey. I accepted his dinner invitation as soon as I made sure that Jana could stay overnight at Laurie's. Then I reluctantly let Terrance into the house and made sure his doggy chow was in his bowl. He made a beeline to it.

As always, Joey arrived dressed to the nines in a three-piece suit, his Cadillac polished almost as brightly as his shoes.

"Who's that?" he pointed to the dog as if he'd never seen anything on four legs before.

"That is Terrance," I answered with strong emphasis on *that*.

"Terrance Who?" he demanded with the infectious laugh that always filled me with joy and made me eager to laugh in return.

When Joey laughed, Terrance suddenly began barking.

"I didn't know he barked," I said in surprise.

"Is he an attack dog?" Joey asked, regarding Terrance with a bit more respect as the dog, still barking, began taking abrupt little lunges back and forth in the space between himself and the laugher.

"No need to worry," I answered, disliking Terrance for still one more reason now that he was being a jerk to my friend. "Unless you're a maple tree or a brown wall-to-wall rug, he'll do you no harm.

"Go lie down," I said sternly, pointing over the dog's head to indicate the kitchen area.

Terrance trotted immediately into the living room and

plunked himself down in the middle of the brown carpet.

"I didn't know you liked dogs," Joey said, evidently impressed at what must have seemed like instant obedience to my command.

"I didn't know I *didn't* like dogs until Terrance," I said as I followed Joey to the door. I shot one last dirty look back at the dog, now basking in the luxury of my brown pile, before I closed the door and locked it behind me.

CHAPTER 3

It was sometime in the middle of the night. I knew immediately that it had to be very late because I had journeyed far up from a deep sleep to stare bewildered into the dark around me. Why was I awake? Something must have drawn me out of my slumber because I'm a good sleeper. I mean, a when-the-head-hits-the-pillow kind of sleeper who stops this side of dying for eight full hours every night.

I was just raising myself so I could see my illuminated clock radio when Franny's voice sailed through my open bedroom window. It was two-thirty in the morning, and I was wide awake because Franny had yelled before. She was calling Terrance in unchecked decibels.

Mortified, I scrambled out of bed so fast that I tripped over the bedsheet, which had somehow gotten twisted around my leg, and pulled half the bedding onto the floor with me when I fell. I was probably lucky that my leg was so encased in sheet and blanket and spread, or I might have hurt myself. As it was, the fall only made me angrier, especially when I heard Franny shrieking Terrance's name again. I had to stop her.

By the time I had grabbed my bathrobe and attempted to wrap it at least partially around my body, she had screamed once more. I raced down the stairs muttering things like, "once a peaceful neighborhood" and "elderly housing violation" and "city codes," and I think my last semi-fathomless utterance was something about "crazy, drunken broads."

At any rate, I had worked my way up to a heated level of hysteria, which I meant to use as impetus when I got hold of Franny and punched her in the face. But I was psychologically unprepared to deal with *Franny's* level of hysteria: it just smacked *me* in the face when I caught the wild look in her eyes. I mean, she was frantic!

"Terrance is gone!" she cried, waving her arms helplessly.

"Gone where?" I asked stupidly. We were both now standing out on the sidewalk in front of my house. She was still dressed to the nines; I was dressed to a minus one.

"Gone," she repeated. "I've looked everywhere."

"Where were you when he ran away?" I asked, thinking she had come home, taken Terrance for a walk, and somehow he'd slipped off the leash.

"At work," she scowled accusingly at me. "You promised you wouldn't let him out."

"I didn't," I said. "He was right here when I went out with Joey. I got back at midnight and went right up to bed. I figured he was asleep somewhere." *Probably in the thickest part of my shag, buried rug-deep,* I wanted to add, but couldn't bring myself to twist the knife already deeply wedged in Franny's heart. "There's no way he could have gotten out," I added simply.

"Maybe Jana knows," Franny suggested hopefully. "Could we wake her?"

"She hasn't seen him. She didn't come home tonight. She stayed across the court at Laurie's because I went out for dinner."

I could have sworn Franny gave me another accusatory look, or maybe I was just getting paranoid.

Franny began crying, breathless spasms interrupting several squeaking sounds she was trying unsuccessfully to conceal.

"Look, Franny, calm down," I said. I was worried she'd hyperventilate. "How far could he have gone, a little dog like that?"

"Someone has probably kidnapped him," she wailed, looking up in despair at the sky and collapsing back into sobs.

"If that's true, they'll return him," I said firmly, "and you'll probably stand to make a good bit of money out of the deal when the dognappers realize their mistake and offer you money to take him back." As I tried to joke, I was also trying to usher Franny back into the house. She evidently was not familiar with O'Henry, or else she was just ignoring my clever reference to "The Ransom of

Red Chief," because she stumbled into the hall still making her squeaking noise.

"Look, go make us some coffee while I have a look around. I know this house better than you do, and I think Terrance has to still be inside. There is no way he could have gotten out without running past me or you when we came in the front door, and he didn't go by me."

Franny nodded weakly. She seemed relieved that I was going to help look for him. It was funny. I had always felt that Franny was independent and assertive, yet here she was, falling apart because of a little hairy creature that liked to intimidate friends and maple trees and pollute shag carpeting. People were difficult to figure out.

It didn't take long to figure out that the dog was not on the main floor. The main floor consisted of only three rooms, the large living room with the north wall totally fireplaced and bricked, the dining room, and the kitchen. There was the tiny half bath off the kitchen, but the door was kept closed. Just the same, I opened it. I snapped on the light. Its handsome red and black décor against the all-white tile floor, walls, and ceiling sprang to life. I loved this bathroom. It was the perfect guest bath, and tonight there were no guests using it, not even four-legged ones.

This meant only one thing, of course. Terrance the Terrible had to be somewhere in one of the upstairs bedrooms, or, God forbid, in one of the closets, and I worried, quite honestly, that I would not be able to resist the impulse to heave him out of a second-story window when I found him.

I had made it explicitly clear that upstairs would be off-limits to any of Franny's friends, and that had included Terrance! Bad enough he should snow all over the main floor; I didn't need the snow belt to be extended to the second level as well. Besides, I just didn't trust the dog. I had horrible pictures in my mind that I would find him under a bed munching on one of my cloche hats, or digging around in a closet he had determined made a perfect indoor sandbox.

What I found was nothing. No mess. Not a thing out of place. No Terrance!

"Did you find him?" Franny's voice called from downstairs.

"No," I yelled down. I didn't try to disguise the bewilderment in my voice.

I stood for a second in the upstairs hall, thinking. He didn't run by me when I came in, and evidently not by Franny, either. If she had been drinking after hours, she certainly didn't show any signs of over-imbibing, and surely not to the point where she would miss seeing her precious dog run into the night. Jana had not taken her keys with her because she was staying the night at Laurie's. So Jana had not carelessly reentered the house and let the dog out. The doors, all steel, with sliding bolts and double locks, had been double-checked before I left, as was my custom. There was no way I was going to walk back into a house at night that had been left unsecured.

Yet the dog wasn't where I'd left him. What had I overlooked?

The more I thought, the more puzzled I became. There was also a vague feeling of unease beginning to gnaw at the edges of my consciousness. I checked under each bed in each room again. I crawled beneath the garments that hung on three sides of my walk-in closet, and pushed everything back in Jana's and Franny's closets. I did the same in the hall closet, peered into the linen closet, and even checked the shower stall in my bathroom and the bathtub in Jana's.

The dog was not in the house!

It was while I tried to compute this indisputable fact that I began to see blue shadows fluttering across the ceiling, first in Franny's room, then in my study next door to it, and finally more shadows joined those even out into the hall where I now stood. What was happening finally hit me with a sickening jolt in my stomach.

"Franny!" I screamed, racing for the stairs and catapulting down to the main floor at least two steps at a time. "You didn't call the police!" I gasped, knowing full well the answer.

Franny was just opening the door, and immediately we were waving in the blue lights of the six cruisers parked in a long line in front of my property.

"I thought it would help," Franny gasped, for once in her life quite obviously speechless. "I didn't need so many; one would have been enough," she said as she stared out at the parade of cars.

This was just too much for me. I was practically numb, I was so angry. First, Franny neglects to tell me that a dog is part of the package until she moves in with it. Then, within a few short hours of their arrival, the old-age home is probably about to circulate petitions to have me thrown out of the neighborhood, my brown carpet is white, my maple tree is decaying, my backyard is developing a barnyard odor, and the entire police department of the city of Southport is now joining hands, arms extended, as they march in perfect precision toward my house—which used to be a quiet and peaceful haven.

"It's a riot squad," Franny whispered, turning in horror to look for my reaction.

"Yes," I said through gritted teeth. "There are twenty-four of them. Six cars, four in a car. Twenty-four."

"Why?" Franny asked. "I called and said we needed a cop at Twelve Grayson Street. I know this town has been trying to beef up the force and make the policemen more appreciated, but this is ridiculous."

"Yes, it is," I agreed. I knew if my face weren't blue, it would be stark white. I was that furious.

"Look, Franny," I said, as if I were talking to one of my delinquent school children, "there's no time to explain adequately. I'm sure one day this subject would have come up in normal conversation, if any normalcy could ever exist with you around. I just didn't see any reason to mention on day one of your stay that there are two major things you must avoid doing while you are here. Don't burn the house down, and don't call the Southport police."

With that, I opened the screen door very slowly, and with no small amount of trepidation, poked my head out. The sergeant in charge left the line and approached me with equal reluctance.

"I'm not armed," I said, feeling like a damned fool. I heard Franny catch her breath from somewhere behind me.

"You got trouble here, Lady?" The cop was one of those hard-nosed types who would not make my embarrassment any easier.

"No, officer, no trouble," I said, anxious to relax him enough so that he'd take his right hand off his gun holster and loosen the white-knuckled grip of his left hand on the strap of his billy club.

"Did you call for a cop? Someone called for a cop," he said.

"A cop," I said, emphasizing the A. "My friend called *a* cop." I should have choked on the word *friend*.

"What's going down here?" he rasped, shifting his feet a bit but not relaxing his defensive posture.

Here it comes, I thought, shifting my own feet a bit, but my shift was like a squirm. "Her dog, ah, got out," I mumbled.

"Beg pardon, Lady?" The sergeant took a half-step closer and cocked his head slightly as a grimace that was more like a sneer spread across his face.

"Her dog seems to be missing," I blurted quickly. I had my eye on his gun hand. For some reason, I had the brief impression that he'd like to shoot me. In all fairness, I really couldn't blame him. At the moment, if I'd been wearing a gun, I might have considered turning it on Franny *and* myself.

I could sympathize with this guy, even as obnoxious as he was, standing there with a backup squad of twenty-three men, stiff in riot position, ready to go to war for their sergeant and their city. I heard one of the men just behind him ask, "What is it, Sarge?"

How many days of abuse, how many jokes would he endure, when they found out it was all about a lost dog?

"Who's in there with you?" the sergeant asked me.

I suppose he was holding out one last strand of hope that the answer would come back Mickey McGadly, an escapee from Walpole this month, or some other notorious person who could save his face.

"Just the two of us," I said. I almost added "Sorry," but thought better of it.

He made some kind of sign to the men because they dropped their arms, and he dropped his hand from the holster and stepped up onto the steps. I held the door open for him to enter. I guessed he wanted to question us further.

For a moment I'd forgotten that I had my ratty-looking bathrobe partially wrapped around me. Now I remembered and tugged at it anew while I gave Franny a sideways dirty look.

She didn't notice. She was gaping at the front door. I turned to watch the entire contingent begin to squeeze into my narrow foyer and spread out slowly into the living room. They weren't going to relax in their job as backup to the sergeant, I supposed. There was a lot to be said for loyalty, but I had a feeling the sergeant would have just as soon been alone on this one.

He took both our names. "Where are the Hapinskys?" he asked.

"They haven't lived here since six years ago," I answered. "You'd think by now the department would know that," I added a little testily.

"I'll be sure to mention it," he said, jotting down something in his notebook.

"Do you want a description?" Franny asked.

I shot her the deadliest glare I could muster.

"A description?" the officer looked at her blankly.

"Of Terrance."

"Terrance Who?" He was grimacing again.

"My dog," she said, ignoring me altogether.

The sergeant threw a quick glance behind him. The men were all congregated in neat little groups, talking. It could have been a cocktail party except for the conspicuous uniforms. I saw one officer bent over my piano, touching one key at a time so lightly that no sound was being emitted. Two other officers were hovered with him as if admiring his musical virtuosity.

"Look, uh, Lady," the sergeant lowered his voice, "you call the pound in the morning. They'll help you."

I saw the tears well up in Franny's eyes. I guess the sergeant did, too. He glanced once more over his shoulder and gestured that we should move into the kitchen.

"What kind of dog is it?" he sighed once we were a few feet away and separated from the others by the kitchen wall.

"A terrier," Franny said eagerly.

"He's white," I said with hostility.

"White terrier," he mumbled into his notebook.

"When and where did you last see him?" the sergeant asked Franny, but I spoke up first.

"He was lying in the living room when I left for dinner tonight—or rather, last night," I corrected. That vague feeling of discomfort began to nag me again.

"Who would have come in while you were out?" the sergeant asked. Suddenly, there was just a hint of interest on his part. He stopped writing.

"No one," I shook my head. I explained about the doors, the keys. I guess I felt like throwing any lifeline to this poor guy, no matter how weak it might be. I could hear the low drone of male voices behind us, and a faint but spirited rendition of "Chop Sticks" was emanating from the piano.

He looked back at the front door, completely solid steel except for a peephole. I took him to inspect the sliding glass door in the dining room, security bar in position as always. He checked the one ground-level window on the main floor. It was locked and had not been tampered with. He made a note and followed me back to the kitchen. I showed him the steel door to the family room downstairs.

He turned the knob, and it opened! He looked at me questioningly. I looked at Franny the same way.

"I didn't open it," Franny said. "It was closed when I came home and started looking for Terrance, and I knew Terrance couldn't go through a closed door. There was no reason for me to check downstairs."

"That door was locked when I left," I said. "And I didn't unlock it before I went to bed."

The sergeant put his hand to his holster and spoke to the nearest officer in a group discussing my hanging spider plant in the hallway. He moved determinedly toward us when his name was called. The others followed.

"Stay here," the sergeant said to us. We stepped back and watched the parade of uniforms move single file through the hallway and around the corner into the kitchen, then snake down the long carpeted cellar stairs to the recreation room. Lights were flicked on as they went, and I could see flashlight beams jumping into what would be shadowy corners and under the long curling bar.

I knew when they'd found the back passageway because I heard their feet scraping on the cement steps that climbed up out of the cellar and into the backyard. Voices came through the back window over the kitchen sink as the men moved around the fenced-in yard flashing their lights under the decks and picnic tables and even into the swimming pool.

"I never thought to look in the swimming pool," Franny moaned. "I'm glad I didn't consider that Terrance might be doing the dog paddle, or worse," she sighed before she began to squeak into her hands.

Only the sergeant returned through the front door, minutes later.

"Your doors at the foot and top of the back cellar stairs that connect to outside were wide open," he said. "So was your gate."

"We never use those doors downstairs," I said, now fully alarmed. "They've been locked for three years, ever since Joe died, and the gate was closed when I left."

"That's probably how the dog got out," the sergeant said.

"But who opened the doors?" I asked, my voice rising. "Were they forced open?"

"No, Ma'am," he said. "I figured it to be the exit, not the entry. I'll have a look around inside. My men are checking the grounds and the garage."

The sergeant was upstairs only a few minutes. "Nothing unusual," he reported when he returned.

I was disappointed. I'd hoped to solve the mystery. Now I'd worry.

"I thought the place was impregnable," I said helplessly.

"It should be," the sergeant agreed, "with those doors of yours. Just keep everything locked up. Maybe it was just a fluke thing, a bolt that wasn't altogether across, or the door not slammed shut in the first place."

I knew he was saying that maybe I had forgotten to secure the place, and that's what gnawed at me. I knew that every door had been locked and bolted as always. If someone had been in here tonight, they knew of an entry that I didn't know about. But that was foolish. How could a house someone had lived in for six years have an unknown point of entry? Still, I knew the place had been totally secured.

I watched the uniformed men move to their respective cars, blue lights now extinguished, and as they pulled away, that vague uneasiness increased perceptibly. I went and checked all the doors one by one, starting with the family-room entries downstairs. Franny helped me, but both of us were now quiet with our own private thoughts and concerns. It did, however, occur to me that it was comforting to have a companion tonight. It also occurred to me that it was Terrance the Terrible who had caused this problem in the first place. . .or was he only the catalyst that had finally exposed a problem that had existed before his arrival? The thought sent a wave of chills down my back, and I quickly buried the idea.

CHAPTER 4

It was five A.M. when we closed the front door behind the cadre of blue- uniformed men. Franny and I stood in the living room peeking out the bay window to watch them go. As they exited the street, at least they didn't use their blue lights, I thought, realizing as I did so that it was small potatoes compared to the damage that probably had already been done. By now, every neighbor, if not convinced I was a woman of ill repute, had no doubt decided that my repute was at least a bit under the weather.

"I didn't know Southport had so many cops," Franny said. "I liked Badge 20. He can raid my house any day." Then she turned and noticed my maniacal expression.

"Franny," I said, trying to keep my mind off strangling her, "let's make some coffee and I'll tell you how I have met every one of these cops, including Badge 20. It is something I apparently should have done before you arrived dog and baggage."

Franny raided the refrigerator while I perked some coffee. By the time I had poured two cups for us, Franny had found and eaten two slices of pizza, half a bag of chips (the jumbo-sized bag), six slices of baloney, half a jar of maraschino cherries, three brownies, and half a grapefruit. In that order!

"It's breakfast time," she said as I regarded the bizarre combination of leftovers incredulously.

"I always eat when I'm worried," she shrugged when I didn't reply.

We changed into shorts and shirts and sat on the top front step with our coffee as the sun came up.

"Just who were the previous owners?" Franny asked when I

had finished telling her the violent history of my house.

"They were Happy's son and family. Happy built this house for them, and they caused nothing but trouble for the poor man, not to mention the embarrassment he must have suffered. They say there was a police raid once a week sometimes, and it was not unusual to see a shotgun poke out of an upstairs window at those times. An uncle who lived with them was always behind the shotgun, so the story goes."

"No wonder the police descended on us in riot formation," Franny gasped, wide-eyed.

"We had a housewarming party the first month after we moved in," I continued, "and about midnight we looked out to behold flashing blue lights everywhere, and then the line of men approaching from the front. We figured some neighbor had complained about a noisy party, and the police hadn't heard that the original owners had sold the house and moved away. They still haven't," I ended, taking a sip of my coffee and studying the dew on my grass as the sun hit it.

"Where could Terrance be?" Franny suddenly sighed. I guess I had managed to take her mind off the dog for a while, and now her worry was back, fresh and therefore more painful.

"He'll show up, Franny. I feel sure of it. My luck has never been at a lower ebb! The more important question to me is, how did he get out?" As she and I mused about our individual questions, Happy pedaled by on his bicycle. He nodded his slow, grand nod as he passed.

"That's Happy," I said to Franny.

"Oh, everyone knows him," she said. "He was a big businessman in this town. He once owned the whole downtown block. Owned the whole damned mall over on Elm."

"I'm going for a walk," I announced, setting my cup on the top step. "Happy makes me feel guilty. Here he is out bicycling at six in the morning."

"Chances are *he* had a few hours' sleep last night," Franny yawned, setting her cup down and rubbing her eyes.

I reached into the hall for my walking shoes, socks from yesterday's walk still in them. One of them! Further investigation on my hands and knees turned the other one up. It had wedged between the sofa and love seat in the living room, the foot still intact, the upper half virtually torn apart. Too lazy to go upstairs for a new pair, I returned to the front steps, picking white hair and brown threads from my reddened knees.

Franny regarded me silently. When I pulled on the tattered sock, it draped limply back down my leg and spilled in segments over my sneaker when I stepped into it.

"I forgot to warn you about shoes and socks," Franny said, dabbing her eyes with a Kleenex she'd retrieved from her bra.

"I don't have pockets," she said to my raised brows.

"What do you think? Franny?" I asked, standing up and facing her. "Should I wear the right sock up or tear it to shreds to match the left one?"

Franny began to bawl.

I felt miserable. I had honestly been trying to make her laugh.

I left her crying on the steps and crossed the street to the sidewalk that wound around the old-age home, my half-mile track, as I called it.

I glanced back at my Colonial in the six A.M. sun. It occurred to me that only twenty-four hours ago, I had sat on those steps where Franny sat crying now. I had been happy then, I sighed, basking in the prospect of a long summer ahead. The question this morning was, could a summer ever last *too* long?

I had only gotten to the other side of the block when a car sped alarmingly fast around the corner up ahead of me and careened down the street right toward me, crossing into the oncoming lane. When I was about to jump for safety into a grove of flowers and trees at the back side of the old-age home, I recognized Dale behind the wheel. He reined in his Pontiac with a screech, nose headed the wrong way into the traffic, inches from where I stood on the sidewalk.

"Does the department know you flunked driver's ed?" I asked.

"I just heard about all the commotion last night," he said, ignoring my sarcasm.

Yes," I nodded, "I imagine the whole town has heard by now."

"What happened?"

I told him, including the part that bothered me most: how the dog had gotten out in the first place.

"You weren't home all night?" His eyes twinkled under brows raised in mockery.

"I went out for dinner, and evidently the dog was missing when I got home, but I didn't notice."

He suggested my daughter may have come home, and I didn't know it. He suggested Franny, whom he knew from the restaurant, had come home a bit more tipsy than she realized, and the animal had gotten out.

I shook my head at both suggestions. "It's something else," I said.

"Look, uh, you teachers get paid over the summer, don't you?"

This sudden change in the conversation surprised me until I saw that he had spotted my drooping sock. I had forgotten about it.

"Franny's dog," I explained.

"It looks like that may be his last victim."

I nodded.

"Franny upset?" he asked.

"I left her hysterical on the front steps just now."

He shifted gears.

"I'll go take a description," he winked, "make her feel better."

"She'll feel better just having you pay attention to her," I said as I waved good-bye. I rather wished that he had stayed to continue our conversation about my worry of last night. On the other hand, I did not want to give him the idea that I was depending on him to defend or protect me. I knew that it would take very little to signal a new plateau in our relationship, simply because of who he was, and I wished to keep that from happening at all costs.

The sock began really bothering me about the third time around the block. It had crept slowly down into the shoe, and since there was nothing to pull except little frayed scraps, I could only let it sink deeper and deeper in a bunch under my heel.

I quit after the third revolution. Besides, I hadn't had much sleep and my muscles knew it. They felt like lead.

I noted that Dale had not talked to Franny long. He had

been gone by the time I'd walked once around the block, and by the time I limped across the street defeated by lack of sleep and sock, Franny was no longer on the front stoop.

I took off my shoes on the steps and threw my socks into the trash barrel in the garage. After hooking up the lawn sprinkler, I went barefooted (my favorite summer state) into the house and poured myself a fresh cup of coffee. I managed to consume the whole thing at my leisure on the front steps as I lazily watched the sprinkler cascading water over my precious grass.

Since I hadn't heard a sound from Franny, I figured she had gone in to get some sleep. It was now eight A.M. She had to be more exhausted than I, since she had worked the night before.

The familiar Mustang appeared at the edge of the courtyard beside me and stopped as he scanned for traffic.

Never me, I sighed. *The macho man with the chest hair never regards me. I've never been looked through so effectively in my life!* I watched the car pull out onto Grayson Street and wondered if a hunk like that could be gay or terribly nearsighted. I realized that my vanity was disgusting, but facts were facts. I was pretty. Men didn't date me for my sexual gifts. The merchandise had been on layaway since Joe died. I was tall, slim, and had a great face. The guy could have at least glanced at me *once* since 1980!

"It pays to advertise," Franny's voice announced from the doorway behind me, and I spun around, stunned for a moment at what must at last be proof of her self-proclaimed extrasensory prowess. She was emerging onto the front steps with a hammer in one hand and a stack of poster board in the other. When I regarded her blankly, Franny propped up the colorful pieces of cardboard, each the size of a small car, against the wrought iron rail and stepped to one side. "What do you think?" she asked with pride in her voice.

HAVE YOU SEEN ME? the posters screamed in dark headlines, and my eyes traveled down to a pathetic picture of Terrance with his scraggly white hair sticking out from every part of his anatomy including his beady little eyes and gaping mouth.

"What are you doing, Franny?" I asked, concentrating on keeping my voice level and low.

"I'm going to spread these around town," Franny said, beginning to count the number of posters.

"You were always good at spreading things around town, Franny," I continued in the same dull tone.

She ignored me, and when she'd counted to fifteen, she began gathering up her materials.

"I guess milk cartons were too small," I said wryly.

Franny gave me a disgusted look and then smirked. "Actually, I thought of adding a message to all the graffiti about me in bathrooms across America, but I decided it would take too long," she said as she started determinedly past me and down the steps. The clumsy pieces of cardboard began to slide around despite Franny's secure grasp.

I sighed and rose slowly. "Here," I said, surrendering to my better nature, "give me a few. I'll help you. You take some in your car, and I'll take some in mine. That way, you'll be done more quickly."

"You're a good friend, Janet," Franny said, scrambling to unload some of her shifting cargo.

"That's correct," I said, accepting four pinks, one green, and three beige sheets, "except that in any truly accurate description of me from now on, one should be sure to include the word *sap!* Or *chump!* Or *jackass*. . ." I continued the litany of moronic nouns all the way into the garage, over to the workbench for a hammer and nails, and into my car.

It was only then that it dawned on me.

"Franny!" I yelled out my window. She was just finishing loading the posters into her back seat and stood for a moment looking into the garage toward my voice.

I stuck my head out the window and said, "Where did you get all that poster board?" Of course, I already knew the answer.

"Oh, I saw it in your den just lying around unused. I hope you don't mind," she said glibly.

I remembered the sweet-talking and conniving I'd had to go through with the art department over the school year, not to mention the time it cost me filling out requisition forms for enough supplies to complete new bulletin board displays over the summer. But I said nothing. I just pulled myself back into the car and thumped my forehead against the steering wheel five times while I waited for Franny to back her car out of the driveway.

CHAPTER 5

I didn't get back to the house for over an hour. When I arrived, Franny was already there working on more posters. She had moved new supplies to the dining room table. I regarded her slouched, concentrated figure for a moment before I spoke.

"Franny," I said, "you've got to be exhausted. Why don't you give it a rest? Fifteen posters are enough for starters. Besides, you've got to sleep or you won't get to work tonight."

"Oh, I called in sick," she said, without looking up from gluing another Xeroxed photo of Terrance to a green poster board.

"Franny—"

"Well, I am," Franny railed at me, and I was dismayed to see fresh tears in her eyes as she finally looked up. "Sick, I mean," she gulped before she started to sob. "Sick at heart," she choked.

"Mom?" The voice called from the foyer just before I heard the screen door click.

"We're in here," I said, feeling miserable and helpless as I reached for a tissue and handed it to Franny.

"What's the matter?" my daughter asked, obviously surprised to see Franny in tears and Terrance all over the dining room table.

"Jana, Terrance is missing," I said as kindly as possible. "Somehow he got out during the night and is nowhere to be found."

"He's got to be somewhere close by," Jana said, going over to put her arm around Franny. "Me and my friends will find him, Franny."

"My friends and I," I corrected.

Jana threw me a look that expressed an entire paragraph about being petty and critical at a time of great misfortune, and then I saw a new expression come over her face.

"Did you let Terrance out, Mom?"

This was too much. My own daughter now regarded me with semi- squeezed-shut eyes and a "don't lie to me" fist on her right protruding hip.

"Jana, I was very careful to lock up the house before I left for the evening," I said, wishing I didn't feel compelled to defend myself to my own child.

I had no idea if she believed me or not because she suddenly went into action. The hip went back into place, and she paced purposefully to the kitchen wall phone. It took her only a half hour to round up every non-adult in the radius of a mile. I had to admit I was impressed with her managerial skills. By two o'clock, she had fanned out a search team carrying Xeroxed pictures. Those who were too young to go trooping through distant neighborhoods either knocked on nearby doors or stayed and helped Franny cut and paste. More poster board was sent for, and a team took a Terrance picture back to the print shop that Franny had used earlier and had another hundred made up. When they told the shopkeeper their story, he did it for free and threw in an extra twenty-five copies besides.

Last night my downstairs had been standing room only for the city police force; now it looked like a day care center—a very populous day care center. Once worried about dog hairs on my carpet, I began worrying about glue and paste and black Magic Marker, not to mention hundreds of dirt deposits from sneakers sized three narrow to ten wide.

By four o'clock, everybody had left to hang the multitude of posters, and I got busy vacuuming. It took a number of sweeps to remove the white dog hairs, which I was convinced had cleverly secured themselves in square knots to every rug fiber on the first floor.

By five, the house smelled of dinner cooking, thanks to my having shoved a roast into the oven earlier, and my downstairs looked normal once more.

"You'd never know a white dog had ever been here," I said to myself, and immediately saw my daughter's suspicious stance and

Franny's tear-stained face in my mind. "I must be a terrible person," I said to the stinging guilt that swept over me. But every time I went into the living room and looked at my clean carpet, I couldn't help it; I felt wonderful!

A disheveled Franny and a disappointed Jana returned sans dog about six o'clock, and made weak overtures to my offerings of steaming roast beef, mashed potatoes, and gravy. For once in her life, Franny just picked at her food.

"I'm going over Laurie's," Jana announced as she rose to carry her still half-filled plate to the kitchen. "Her dad has a CB radio, and he's going to help us put out the description on all the major channels. Don't worry, Franny, we'll have Terrance home before it's dark."

This last prediction was made as my daughter gave Franny a confident pat on the back and both of us a preoccupied wave good-bye. I was glad I had stopped myself before I corrected her "over Laurie's" to "over *to* Laurie's," or reprimanded her failure to be excused from the table. I heard the screen click behind her departure and her running feet in a hurry to reach Laurie and the CB radio, and knew, for the moment, that her heart was in the right place.

"Well," I sighed to Franny, scraping back my chair, "give me time to clean up and I'll walk around the neighborhood with you before it gets dark."

"You don't have to, really," she said weakly. But she got up with me from the table and helped me clear. By the time I had the roast put away and the pans cleaned, it was seven-thirty and the sun was beginning to move into its setting stance over Martha's house.

I heard Franny come back into the kitchen behind me. "Okay," I said, wiping my hands one last time, "where to?"

I turned and regarded Franny, who had sunk into a kitchen chair with a posture that mirrored her despair. She had a few posters that she had let slide from her lap and onto the floor.

"Don't give up now," I told her. "You've got an army out looking, and they'll find him." I wanted to doubt my words, but Franny suddenly braced up, and grabbing her posters, headed for the door.

I locked up quickly and joined her on the front steps. "We haven't been around on the other side of the old-age home and then to the left, toward Brooksville," Franny directed when we started walking.

"Oh," I said, shaking my head to indicate understanding, "by the boarded-up houses," and immediately wanted to take back my words. Franny's overactive imagination once took us an hour out of our way following what she was convinced were lights from a landed flying saucer. The green haze had turned out to be glowing greenhouses on top of an isolated ridge. They were eerie all right, but not extraterrestrial.

Now I held my breath and waited for the inevitable string of queries about the strange houses, but Franny didn't even comment as she handed me a couple of posters which had begun to slip from her grasp, and we moved in silence along the street.

"I'm worried about you, Franny," I finally said, and meant it.

"I'll be fine," she shrugged, "just as soon as we find Terrance."

I hated the knowledge that I felt fine so long as we *didn't* find Terrance. That's probably why, for the next hour, I threw myself completely into the task of pinning posters to trees and telephone poles up and down Sawyer Boulevard.

We were literally nailing the last poster to the last pole when Franny suddenly paused in midflight of her hammer and looked around.

"Do you hear it?" she asked me.

I listened, straining my ears to hear past the sound of the light traffic along the street where we stood. It was now close to dark, and houses all along the way had lamps glowing behind their screened windows. It had been a warm day, and the gentle breezes stirred curtains at those screens and felt cool to my bare arms and legs.

"I hear a dog barking in one of the houses nearby," I said, looking questioningly at Franny.

I could make out lines of intense concentration on Franny's face even in the rapidly descending darkness.

"It's Terrance!" Franny said. Her voice was barely a whisper as she spun first to the right, then the left, trying to be sure of the direction.

"Franny, you're tired; it's late; you haven't really slept for going on two days; let's go home." I took the hammer from her and finished banging the nail into the poster.

Franny still hovered, listening.

"It's Terrance," she said again, this time in a quiet voice. "It's coming from there!" She pointed toward the corner where I knew one of the boarded-up houses stood.

"Franny, you're tired," I tried again, the beginning of helpless dread starting to flicker in the pit of my stomach.

"I know Terrance when I hear him," she said in a louder voice now, one tinged with anger at my obvious doubt.

"Hear that? Gr-r-r-r! and then the yips. That's Terrance's voice," she nodded confidently. "Gr-r-r-r yip; gr-r-r-r yip," she mocked the sound again.

I stood looking at her incredulously.

"Franny, he's a terrier. All terriers sound the same," I chided.

"It's Terrance. He's in that house," she said, starting toward what should have been a front walk.

I already knew that there was no opening in the high hedge that obscured the entire house front. I also knew that the hedge ran uninterrupted along the front of the house next door to the one Franny wanted access to. I had studied both houses for as long as I had done my walking routine. I had found them strange, especially lately, when I had come to realize that they were occupied. In the middle of a busy city, two very large Colonials were boarded up but occupied! It was certainly curious. So curious that I had questioned Dale about it. He had shrugged, said it was some kind of legal standoff about building permits, and had dismissed the topic.

What Franny also didn't know was that the man who apparently lived in one house and the women who occupied the other were as strange as their living conditions. It had become clear to me that they moved freely and often between the two houses, concealed by the high hedge from passersby but not from me as I walked my circuit on the other side of the wide boulevard at five AM. From that vantage point, I had a clear view over the hedge and onto both properties.

There were at least two women; both looked old. One had long bleached hair, and the other, seemingly older, had glasses and a short dark bob. When they went off the property, the blonde always drove with the elder one in the back seat. The man had his own car, but both cars were old Studebakers from the fifties and were kept in the double garage under the first house, the house Franny was headed for now.

"Franny," I was whispering loudly when I caught up to her. "What are you going to do?"

"I'm going to knock on the door as soon as I find my way around the hedge," she answered irritably. "Terrance is in that house. I will not leave here until I have him out of the hands of whoever stole him. They can't just grab my dog and think they'll get away with it!"

"Franny, you're mistaken," I gasped, but not as loudly as Franny gasped when we reached the end of the hedge by the garage doors. For at that point, Franny could see the boards placed solidly over the front bay windows and the smaller side windows.

"These are vacant houses!" Franny blurted. "Somehow Terrance has gotten trapped inside. . ."

Her voice trailed off, and I followed her gaze to the second story. A light shone from the only window not boarded up, an upstairs side window over the garage. This window was open and, I figured, screened in order to allow the summer night breezes entry. Franny studied the lighted window for a few seconds and then turned her gaze on me. In the now complete darkness of night and hedge, I could not see her expression clearly, but I could imagine that it was one that demanded answers.

"I don't understand either," I assured her. "These houses have been here just as you see them for as long as I remember, but they are not unoccupied. This one and the one next door have tenants. They're strange people who keep to themselves, except sometimes you see them driving by in cars as strange as they are and—"

"Terrance is in there," Franny cut me off and disappeared into the darkness.

I knew there were white cement steps up to a regular front

door. I had seen the man come out of that door a few times during my early-morning walks. Now, I held my breath and listened to the rustle of Franny's steps across what I knew was a weed-infested front lawn. The dog had ceased its barking some time ago.

I waited for the inevitable sound. I cringed when it came.

Whomp! Whomp! Whomp! Franny must have used her whole body's momentum to achieve such thunderous cacophony as her fist crashed against the wooden door. Immediately, the sound of a dog barking began again, and it was from somewhere inside the house. My eyes flew upward in time to see the lighted window on the second floor go dark. Now, only the streetlights gave any kind of illumination.

Whomp! Whomp! Whomp! Franny knocked again.

Silence, except for the dog! I crept slowly, carefully, toward what must be the front door, based on my memory of Franny's rapping.

Deeper into the front yard, it became darker as I moved and put the hedge between me and the streetlamps. I was ducking slightly, aware that whoever had dowsed the light in the upstairs room could see me until I cleared the side of the house, and even then it was impossible to know if the boarded windows were solid or if slits or cracks, accidentally or by design, allowed one on the inside a peephole to the front lawn.

Whomp! Whomp! Whomp! Franny knocked a third time.

I was able to make out her form, darker than the white cement steps, just before she started screaming.

Whomp! Whomp! Whomp! "I know my dog is in there!"

Whomp! Whomp! Whomp! "Terrance, it's Mommy!"

Whomp! Whomp! Whomp! "Open this door! I want my dog! Terrance, it's Mommy!"

Whomp! Whomp! Whomp! "Open this door or I'll get the police! Do you hear me? I'll bring the police!"

I managed then to get to her. She was heavy and solidly built, but by now she was sobbing again, and her emotions had finally weakened her resolve, thank goodness. I was able to steer her slowly off the cement platform and down the three steps to the unkempt lawn, then step by step across the darkness behind the hedge and back to the side street. I imagined eyes on us all the way, especially across the lighted boulevard, and I didn't breathe a relieved sigh until we were around the corner of the old-age home and on the Grayson Street side. I had been talking her along, soothing kinds of innocuous things like, "We'll go home now; you'll feel better; just a bit more and we'll be home. . ."

The phone was ringing when I unlocked the front door. It was Jana. "Where have you been?" she asked without the courtesy of a hello back to mine.

I didn't explain. It suddenly hit me that this whole ugly twenty-four hours had suddenly taken an even uglier turn. What had started as a carefree opening to a long relaxing summer vacation had careened into the grotesque black-and-white portrait of Franny hysterically beating her fist on a neighbor's door. A strange neighbor, granted, but Franny was strange, herself. She was, I concluded, out of control. And over that pathetic excuse for a dog!

"Mom? Are you all right?" Jana broke into my reverie.

"It's been a long day," I mumbled.

"I think I may have good news for Franny," her voice was tinged with a quality I didn't hear very often lately. She was really concerned. Perhaps when this purgatory of adolescence was over, she'd emerge a pretty decent human being.

"She could use some," I said, looking around the corner to make eye contact with Franny, who had collapsed in a living room chair when we came in. The chair was empty. Feelings of dread resurfaced immediately. I pictured chasing Franny back to that abominable house, dark and boarded and downright weird.

"Laurie's father talked to a guy on the CB who says a dog of Terrance's description was picked up last night by the dog catcher."

"He'd be at the pound, then," I said, looking at the clock. It was past nine.

I realized the alternative to chasing Franny around the neighborhood again might be if I could persuade her (if I could find her) to go down to the pound. I told Jana we'd check it out.

"I'll stay at Laurie's till you get back," Jana suggested. "Could you pass me a dollar over the fence? We want to get an ice cream."

I pictured Jana and all her friends working so hard all day and decided ice cream was certainly reasonable. I hung up and took two dollars out of my purse, shouting to Franny that I'd be right back. No one answered me.

I hurried out the back way through the slider, not even stopping to put on the deck light. When I reached the bottom step I could see Jana just coming out of Laurie's across the court. I hurriedly found my way around the pool and stood on tiptoes to peek over the fence. Jana had been waiting and dashed across the narrow street that separated our property from Laurie's. She whispered a fast thank-you as she took the bills. I waited long enough to watch her safely back across the court, and was turning to retrace my steps and go looking for Franny when movement at the yard next door to Laurie's caught my eye.

I stood up on tiptoes again just as Laurie's porch light went off. It didn't matter. In the thin glow from the streetlight, I could make out my macho man deep in the shadows by the side of his house. His arms were flailing in what appeared to be an intense conversation with a woman, a short, overweight woman; a woman built just like Franny. It was, in fact, Franny!

I watched, hypnotized, as she gestured in the direction of my house, and he leaned into her face and shook her by the shoulders. There were no voices. Whatever they were arguing about, they were doing it in whispers that didn't reach my ears.

I fled back around the pool and up the steps of the deck. By the time I had secured the slider, I was breathing heavily, not from the short distance I had traveled, but from my reaction to the bizarre scene I had just witnessed. How did Franny know my neighbor, and what in the world were they so embattled about?

I paced and tried to get hold of myself. Why was I so upset? Was it just one too many strange episodes in the last day and a half and my last straw?

I heard Franny let herself into the foyer and marched across the living room to meet her.

"Where did you disappear to?" I asked, trying not to sound as hysterical as I felt.

"I walked around the neighborhood one last time," Franny answered reasonably.

"I didn't know you knew the man who lives in the house next to Laurie's," I blurted with a Jana squint to my eyes and an edge to my voice.

Franny looked quickly at me and then away. "What man?" she asked, moving toward the kitchen.

I pulled Franny over to the window above the sink that faced the pool and the courtyard beyond. "The man in *that* house," I said, spitting out the word *that* and jabbing a finger toward the green house. "The one you were just talking to."

"Oh," Franny said, nodding nonchalantly. "I was asking him if he'd seen Terrance."

"The hell you were," I snarled.

Franny glanced at me strangely, I thought, and sank into a chair at the table.

"I'm exhausted," she sighed. "I've got to go to bed."

"What's his name?" I asked, realizing I really was dying to know it.

"Who?" Franny asked blankly.

"The guy in the green house," I practically shouted.

"I don't think he said," she shook her head and squinted as if she were really trying to remember.

"Franny, what is going on? Are you and this guy seeing each other?"

"You jealous?" An old Franny smile began to curl her lips.

"As a matter of fact, I think I am. I've been eyeing that guy for years. Who is he?"

"He didn't say," replied Franny with a perfectly sober expression once again.

"What's the use?" I sighed, throwing my arms into the air and dropping into the chair opposite her. "All I can say is, if he's your latest, your taste in men has improved tremendously."

Franny gave me another look that I thought for a moment showed a bit of merriment, like the old Franny would have shown me before she got emotionally involved with a dog.

"Look, Franny, Jana says a terrier fitting Terrance's description (don't they all)," I injected, "was picked up by the pound. I'll drive you over if you want to check it out."

Franny was on her feet and heading for the door before I'd finished the sentence.

"I guess she wants," I nodded to the air, and went to lock up the house yet again and catch up with her.

CHAPTER 6

The pound was an addition onto the police station. A familiar-looking officer with jowls like a bulldog looked at us grudgingly as we interrupted his game of solitaire. He gave Franny a double-take, and I realized he had been one of the officers mingling in my living room the night before.

"We'd like to see your dogs," Franny said sweetly.

"Not my dogs, Lady. I hate the filthy critters," he grumbled as he rose with great lethargy from his chair and pulled a ring of keys off a wooden peg.

Franny was wringing her hands, and I knew she'd be terribly disappointed if Terrance wasn't there. I, of course, had mixed feelings. If the dog were found, I'd have difficulty dealing with Franny because I had not agreed to a four-legged tenant, and the last day and a half had convinced me that I should have dealt with the situation initially. If the dog were not found, dealing with Franny would be just as unpleasant in other ways.

Bulldog ushered us through a small door in the back wall and led us into a long corridor to another small door. By now we could hear dogs barking. I glanced at Franny to see if she heard any familiar *gr-r-r-r yips*.

"Filthy and loud," Bulldog muttered as he opened the second door.

Cages lined the cement-floored room and stretched the length of a football field.

"Isn't he precious?" Franny cooed at a poodle with a pink bow behind its right ear in the first cage.

"That your dog, Lady?" snarled the officer, beginning to insert a key into the cage's lock.

"No, no," Franny corrected him. "My dog is a terrier."

"A white West Highland Terrier," I added, truly trying not to accentuate the word *white*.

The officer withdrew his key as he glared at Franny. "This here ain't no pet store, Lady. Never mind browsing. Is your dog here or ain't he?"

Franny began moving along the passageway, peering eagerly into each cage. I was beginning to hold my breath. One part of me suddenly wanted Terrance to be there—the masochistic side of me, I was sure.

The officer began to look at his watch. "We close in five minutes," he muttered.

Franny nodded solemnly and kept moving.

Suddenly she let out a little gasp and rushed over to a huge black-and-brown St. Bernard in a pen across the room. "Big Boy!" She chirped, and began clapping her hands with great enthusiasm. "Is that you, Big Boy?"

I had reached her side now. "Franny," I whispered, "what are you doing?"

"One of the guys at the restaurant lost his Saint Bernard last week. I think this is Bert's dog."

The officer's growl, as he caught up to us, was louder than those of the fifty dogs chorusing in the background. "What the hell you trying to pull, Lady? That dog ain't no terrier; hell, he ain't even white!"

"Let's get out of here," I said, casting a hateful look back at the officer, who followed us out cursing.

"Next time, try Pets Are Us over on Maple and Elm," I heard him yell before I got the door closed behind us.

When I reached home, I called Jana at Laurie's and snapped on the spotlights to guide her home. "Unless you'd like to call your handsome friend to escort her from the court," I suggested to Franny. She completely ignored me except to throw me a dirty look.

It turned out that Jana had an escort after all. "Mom! Franny!" we heard her yelling from the corner of the house. "Terrance is back! Mom! Franny, look who's home!"

Sure enough, as we rushed to the door, there he was in all his whiteness, wiggling and wagging up the front steps and into the freshly vacuumed foyer.

CHAPTER 7

We got a good night's sleep that night; at least we all got a chance to sleep through for the first time in the two days since Franny had moved in. It was eleven when we retired, and though there were no disturbances, I slept fitfully and found myself fully awake with the first hint of dawn at the sides of my curtains. I got up and pulled on some shorts and a T-shirt, found new and whole socks, slid comfortably into my sneakers, and with a rush of delight, let myself out noiselessly into a quiet five A.M. morning.

As I walked, I attempted to sort out all the pieces and details of the last two days that had been hurling themselves around in my head during the night and causing me to drift in and out of a shallow sleep. Each time I circled the Sawyer Boulevard side of the old-age complex and studied the boarded-up houses, I remembered they'd had a part in my dreams, as well as the image of a hysterical Franny pounding on their boards until they fell silently apart to expose a white shaggy dog.

Last night as I had watched a tearful Franny greet her lost Terrance, I recalled the threat she had screamed a couple of hours before the dog materialized on the sidewalk in front of our house, where Jana, returning home, had found him.

How had he gotten there, and did Franny's warnings about bringing the police to the strange house have anything to do with his returning when he did?

In the growing light of morning, I studied the houses as if I would find an answer if I stared at them long enough.

Why would anyone kidnap a dog? Especially that dog! Was I really ready to believe that Franny had been able to recognize

Terrance's bark inside that strange hermitage? And if she had been so convinced that he was in there, why had she bothered to go to the pound last night on the tip that Jana had given me? Was that simply a desperate attempt to cover all the possibilities?

I had circled my half-mile track three times before I observed any activity at the houses in question. A man, the same tall, middle-aged man I had seen on previous occasions, came out the front door of the house on the left and crossed the front lawn, heading in the direction of the double garage on the side of the house on the right. As he rounded the second house, the left garage door opened and the purple Studebaker backed slowly out into the driveway and stopped. The man bent forward briefly toward the driver's window and then stepped back, and the car continued its reverse direction to the street.

By now, I was about to turn the corner at Sawyer Boulevard, and at the pace I was moving, would have my back to the car and its projected path unless I changed from my usual course.

So I did. I wanted to get a good look at the occupants in that ugly Studebaker. I stopped at the curb, looked deliberately both ways and crossed ever so slowly to the opposite sidewalk on the boulevard just as the car pulled up to the stop sign right beside me. I looked through the rolled up driver's window into the eyes of a woman with a long, harsh face surrounded by thick yellow hair. Just as she moved the car out onto the street, my eyes darted to the back window. I saw a form huddled against the side of the rear seat, and then the car was behind me and gone. I didn't turn to look again because now I was opposite the garage. The man was nowhere to be seen, and both garage doors were now down.

I turned around and went back to the boulevard and crossed to my usual sidewalk to pick up my regular walking route. I kept wondering where two old women might be headed at five-thirty in the morning. I couldn't believe the stooped figure in the back seat had a job, and it was too early for a church service this Sunday morning, wasn't it? The whole situation seemed strange to me. Two houses in the city boarded up with strange characters coming and going from a garage shared by the people in both of the homes. . . . And the cars, too unkempt to be valuable antiques, yet antiquated by at least thirty years. . . .

My musings were interrupted as I turned the corner and started down my own street. A familiar white dog, his leash dragging behind him, was making a beeline across Grayson and straight at me.

"Terrance," I said, stopping to intercept him as he reached me, "what are are you doing loose?" I made an attempt to grab his leash, but he had decided this would be a good time to play and did a clever sideways maneuver that left him rolling around on the green grounds of the old-age home and me teetering on the brink of joining him.

"Terrance, come here," I tried again, clapping my hands and making stupid sucking sounds with puckered lips. Terrance stopped rolling and jumped to his feet, thrusting his fanny straight up in the air and flattening his front legs against the grass. There he froze, staring at me.

"Terrance," I said, putting my hands on my hips, "you're interrupting my walk. I hate that. It won't count so much, aerobically speaking."

Terrance issued a low guttural growl and did a single leap upwards as if his legs were on springs, and then resumed his previous rear-end salute.

I could feel my Irish temper kick in. It said, "For God's sake, ignore the creepy little dog and do your walk." Which is what I did. The hell with Terrance and his cutesy game.

I started past him, and out of the corner of my eye, I saw him spring toward me just before I felt my right sock being ripped away from my leg. Terrance had stopped me in my tracks and was now purposely devouring a second sock with me in it! His head was pivoting back and forth as he stuffed the sock deeper behind his sharp little teeth, all the while emitting low growls I imagined to be of doggy ecstasy.

I did the only thing my Irish indignation would allow: I kept walking, albeit dragging Terrance. I figured if I reached down to pull him off, he might mistake my hand for the sock and ruin my handwriting and piano playing for a long time.

Take a step, drag Terrance! I tried, against my better subconscious voice, to kick the dog in the teeth, but I couldn't get good balance or enough distance between his teeth and my foot to cause much pain. And right now, I wanted to give Terrance a lot of pain.

I visualized the old people who rose early riveted behind their almost-closed curtains, having a great time over the scene Terrance and I were playing out for them.

Just as I had finally stopped my walking effort entirely and had begun scanning the ground for a stick, or better still, a substantial rock with which to beat the dog's brains out, the air was pulverized by a high-pitched whistle. Both Terrance and I looked up to see Franny standing on the porch steps, her legs braced apart, her hands, with forefingers still extended, just coming away from her mouth, where she had placed them to execute her famous whistle-like-a-man impression.

The dog, without regard for traffic, sprang across the street, up the walk and steps, and into Franny's waiting arms. I looked down at my shredded sock and gave up on the idea of resuming my activity, at least until I could change.

Franny was inspecting the leash as I limped up the walk. "I forgot to tell you how good he is at escaping from his restraints," she said.

I put my right foot up on the top step and stopped. "Don't worry, Houdini," I spoke through gritted teeth to the dog nestled against Franny's ample bosom, "now I have a matching pair."

When Franny had resecured Terrance in the dog run, she found me on the front steps with my first cup of coffee.

"I'll get you a couple new pairs of socks," she said by way of apology. "Caldor's has a three-for-two sale all week."

"Buy several pairs," I suggested, "and we'll feed Terrance a sock or two a day, straight. That way it will cut down on personal injury. His and mine!"

"Look," Franny said, "I know this arrangement isn't working out. I've made inquiries, and a place should become available to me in a few days. Can I stay until I find a suitable room?"

I sighed a long sigh. "Franny, you can stay as long as you want. It's that miserable little hairy deformity you call Terrance that's the issue here. Why would you neglect to tell me you had such an aggravating appendage in the first place?"

"I don't know," Franny shrugged. "I guess I didn't think he'd be a problem."

I looked at her incredulously. "The dog isn't a *problem*, Franny. He goes *beyond* problem. He goes into the echelons with such things as contagions, conflagrations, plagues, and locust infestations! You should have told me," I ended, feeling rotten that my anger had built up to this point. I really liked Franny despite what I considered to be a gross misrepresentation and advantage-taking on her part.

Franny was nodding silently, staring straight ahead and not at me.

"And another thing," I said, figuring I might as well speak truthfully about everything that was bothering me now that I was on a roll, "tell me how you know the guy in the green house behind us." I turned to look Franny in the face. "If you're going out with him, just say so. What's the big deal? Why would you lie about it?"

"I don't know him," Franny said and continued to stare straight ahead.

Their intense conversation under cover of darkness flashed into my mind as I looked at her. I knew she was lying! But why?

"What's the big deal about this guy to you?" Franny threw my words back at me and finally turned to regard me with narrowed eyes.

"I think I'm getting a stupid crush on him," I confessed, surprising myself with my blatant honesty. "No, I think I've been developing a stupid crush for a long time, but if he's your friend, I'll undevelop it, gladly. He seems like a nice guy, Franny. I'd like to see you date a nice guy instead of the questionable characters you've usually been attracted to."

"I've been involved with nice guys before," Franny argued defensively.

"Well, the ballerina was okay, I guess." I began taking closer stock.

"Oh," Franny emitted a sound that was half gasp and half laugh, "he was such a sexual deviate! I mean, I couldn't get into trapezes and onto balance bars; I'm not built for those kinds of activities."

"I don't want to know about any of this," I interrupted her. "All I asked about was the guy next door."

"I don't know him," Franny said flatly, staring straight ahead again, and I knew that was the end of the conversation.

Why would a woman who would gladly have shared any perverted information I might wish not to know about, lie to me about knowing a neighbor of mine? But lying she was; I was sure of it!

"Mom," a somewhat authoritative voice said suddenly from the upstairs bedroom window, "do you have any idea what time it is?"

I looked up at the sun hovering now over the well-kept Peddington house to the left of the old-age home. "Still early, Honey," I said. "You can sleep a little longer."

"Mo...om," the voice was now clearly disgusted, "we're doing an earlier mass today, remember?"

I'd forgotten! Jana had been invited to go for an overnight in Rockland with Laurie and her family. Their departure time was noon today, the time we normally caught the late mass.

"Okay, Hon." I scrambled to my feet. "We'll make the eight o'clock, don't worry."

"Mothers!" I heard her mutter as she backed away from the window.

"I'm going to spend the day organizing my room," Franny told me as she followed me inside. There was a sigh in her voice. "No sense to unpack completely. I'll try to categorize things into what I'll need for the next few days and what can now stay packed."

I didn't comment. What was there to say? I was truly sorry that this move had not worked out.

Jana was dressed and blowing her hair dry when I got upstairs. I showered quickly, pulled my hair back and stuck a wide-brimmed hat on my head to camouflage my uncoiffured hairdo. The hat complemented my light-green summer dress and my already modest tan. I added a dab of mascara and light pink lipstick, and we were off.

Jana and I always walked the short three blocks to the tiny brick chapel unless the weather was bad. Today, soft warm breezes lightly teased my hat. I could smell the ocean on their breath. "It will be a glorious day to go to Rockland," I told Jana, who bounced along beside me in the new nylons and tiny-heeled shoes she had bought for the trip. She was maturing so quickly. I was suddenly aware of how confidently she carried herself. Laurie's family was having a reunion today, and then tomorrow they had promised the children a trip to Great Lake Park before returning home tomorrow night.

Jana turned toward me to start to tell me something when I saw her look out of the corner of her eye and then take a sharp breath.

I turned around and beheld a white streak bearing down on us at great speed. Terrance!

"It's Terrance!" we gasped in unison.

"Save your nylons if you can," I warned her.

I really thought the crazy little dog would hit us dead-on at forty miles an hour, but in the last few seconds before impact, he veered around us and raced in a circle at our feet. We were now standing perfectly still, stupidly rotating our heads to study his orbit. He continued to circle us until he must have found his brake pedal, but then, having slowed, he started jumping at first Jana and then me. The two of us began a chorus of "Down, Terrance!" and finally Jana managed to quiet him somewhat by clamping a hand around the back of his neck and pushing his face close to the sidewalk. I would have pushed his face *into* the sidewalk had I gotten hold of him first.

"Now what do we do?" Jana asked me, looking up from her bent-over position.

"It's too late to take him back," I said. "He'll have to stay loose until after church."

"But what if he runs away again?" Jana asked with sincere worry in her voice.

"He'll see us go into church, and he'll wait for us to come out," I said. I sounded sure of myself, but I wasn't. Jana must have believed it because she didn't argue when I started walking again.

I was honestly surprised that Terrance trotted along beside us with a semblance of decorum.

When we reached the foot of the church steps, I turned and looked down at him. In my best school-teacher voice, I commanded him to stay. Jana added, with a hint of baby talk, that we wouldn't be long.

The dog actually looked like he was listening. He tilted his head first at me when I was talking and then at Jana when she had her say. But I didn't like his expression. To me he looked shifty, like he was up to something.

But then, what did I know? The wretched little mutt was making me crazy. The fact that I was entertaining the notion that the dog had facial expressions, let alone logical thought processes, suddenly scared the hell out of me.

We left the critter there on the sidewalk to contemplate anarchy and entered the chapel. The procession was forming in the vestibule, and we ducked around them and hurried over to the far left of the church where we found an empty pew halfway down.

We barely had time to say a quick prayer before the organ tooted three rapid chords which signaled the congregation to stand. Down the center aisle they came. The altar boy carrying the cross was first in the procession, followed by the reader, who held the Lectionary high above his head so everyone could see the gold cross emblazoned on its red cover. Old but elegant in his silky vestments, Monsignor McCrary followed a line of other altar attendants, the choir director, and the entire choir marching two abreast.

And then came Terrance!

Terrance was the only one in the procession not singing "Amazing Grace," but he was prancing along smartly as if he knew exactly where he was going and what his mission would be once he got there. I stopped singing, and Jana and I looked at each other with fear on our faces.

When we looked back at the center aisle, the procession had arrived at the altar and was climbing the three plushly carpeted stairs to its floor. Terrance was still there climbing with them. For a few seconds everyone in line was busy scattering to their assigned stations and didn't see the creature who trailed them. Monsignor, moving slowly as always in specially cushioned slippers to protect his arthritic feet, had not reached the final steps to the edge of the altar.

As Terrance found himself on a higher level, he turned and surveyed the congregation. You could hear the tittering ripple through the church. Some guy in back of me muttered that it was about time someone besides Monsignor gave the sermon.

Just as Monsignor would have turned to catch a glimpse of the invader, one of the choir members whispered a loud, "Shoo!" and Terrance, startled, did a quick exit from the altar, partly running, partly tumbling over himself and rolling off the three stairs, whereupon he made a frantic dash into one of the first pews way over to our right.

"Why don't you just quietly go and coax him outside? He'll follow you," I suggested into Jana's ear.

"Me!" She jabbed a forefinger into her heart. "Why don't you? He minds you better than me."

"I never saw that dog before in my life," I said and picked up the hymnal for the final verse of "Amazing Grace."

Jana shrugged and followed my lead, and we both kept the books in front of our noses while our eyes bounced back and forth off the horizons of our peripheral vision.

We watched in horror as the dog systematically entered and loped down each pew on the right side. By the time he had reached the left side, he'd become frenzied in his frustration to find us, and he began bounding down the length of the seats and leaping over feet. We could hear gasps and giggles and scuffing noises and even a few muffled shrieks. I winced, imagining nylons being ripped by doggie toenails.

"Look at him book it," Jana giggled into her cupped hand.

"You book it," I said in disgust, jabbing my finger into her missal.

Terrance had just nosedived into what I estimated to be pew number twenty-three, about ten pews down from where we sat in fear and trepidation, when he disappeared. I mean, the noise of feet and dog and shifting bodies ceased abruptly.

"Someone just killed him," Jana whispered.

"I'll pray for his tick-infested soul," I muttered. But I began to wonder just where the little varmint had disappeared to. I would have preferred a warning that he was about to close in on us. I had decided that when he had advanced by five more pews, I would grab Jana and attempt to make a dignified getaway. But at this juncture, there was not a hint of any four-legged intruder. Monsignor had launched into the homily and every feather in every hat, every particle of dust in the air, was at peace.

Monsignor gave a mercifully short discourse, because of the warm and enticing weather he said, but I knew the heat was bothering him from the many times he paused to wipe his brow with his white handkerchief.

By the middle of his homily, Jana and I had begun to relax. We looked at each other every so often with a puzzled frown and a who-knows (in my case, who-cares) shrug. I couldn't explain Terrance's sudden vanishing act, and I wasn't going to dwell on our good fortune. Perhaps there was a compassionate God who shared my distaste for one of his more flawed creations.

At any rate, I wasn't expecting another Terrance outburst when it did finally occur. Monsignor had just faced the congregation and lifted his arms to begin the Nicene Creed. "We believe," he was praying, "in one God. . ."

Out of pew number twenty-three where he had disappeared ten minutes earlier, tore Terrance. In his haste, he bolted across the aisle and dove into the pew on the opposite side of us.

". . .the Father Almighty. . ." Monsignor continued, eyes bulging at the sight of the unexpected streak across the aisle.

Terrance almost immediately tripped and fell or was tossed out of the pew because he landed on his nose with a painful yip, and then began to streak around the church, building quickly to the familiar breakneck speed that had propelled him down the street after us.

". . .maker of Heaven and. . .Earth," Monsignor recited haltingly as he began to track the streak around the aisles with his eyes only.

By the time Terrance had begun his trek down the center

aisle a second time, the dog was churned up for a marathon record. His chin, ears, and hair flipped up and down above seemingly elasticized legs. He was headed straight toward Monsignor on the altar.

". . .of all that is seen. . ." gasped the Monsignor, eyes about as large as I'd ever seen in anyone before.

At the last minute, Terrance did a square turn, mostly skidding on his chin, and charged up the right front, disappearing as he raced up the side aisle again.

Monsignor, arms still raised, now raised his 6'4" frame as far as he could upon his toes to keep his eyes on Terrance. ". . .and unseen," he said, dropping his voice and his heels back to his regular position.

Just then a scuffle began at the back of the church, and the entire congregation turned, as one body, and observed a burly usher wrestling with a thrashing bundle of hair. The hair was snarling.

"Terrance is snarling," Jana whispered unnecessarily.

"I knew that behind that cutesy 'look at me, I'm a darling puppy' routine lurked the soul of a killer," I muttered under my breath.

The snarling escalated as the front door was opened and Terrance had a moment to ponder his fate. Then the big doors closed with a resounding clang, and all was at peace once more.

Monsignor hadn't missed a beat while the animal show was going on; in fact, I suspected that he had seized the opportunity to skip over a few parts while the congregation was distracted, because we were suddenly on our feet singing "Holy! Holy! Holy!"

It was then that we both noticed Dicky Dunlap waving from the now-famous pew twenty-three. It was difficult to guess how long he had been trying to get our attention. The sixteen-year-old had been our neighbor for years, and I always kidded Jana about the crush I suspected he had on her. Jana always called him a dork. I wasn't quite sure what Webster would have said the word meant, but I was sure from Jana's tone when she said it that Dicky's love must be unrequited.

"Oh, God." It was Jana's turn to mutter as she put a defensive hand over her forehead as if to shield her eyes. "Now everyone will hear about how Dicky came to my rescue to save my dog."

"Franny's dog," I corrected and stuck my burning face into the missal.

"I knew it was your dog," Dicky boasted to Jana and me. He was breathless from bolting up the aisle after mass ended in an effort to catch up to us. "I owed you one for missing the poster alert. I just started patting him, and he calmed right down," he bragged. There was immense pride in his voice. "I'd have kept it up, too, except he started squirming, and I couldn't hold him without using some of my karate moves." Dicky did a few quick jabs with his forearms, elbows extended, and I saw Jana roll her eyes to the top of her head as she increased her walking speed.

"He'll have it blabbed all over the place about how my dog acted like such a retard in church," Jana moaned after Dicky had left us at his corner. "He's such a jerk. How will I ever face my friends?"

My daughter's reaction was beginning to gnaw at my nerves. "Tell them the truth. Tell them he's not your dog," I said, aware that my voice did not hold much, if any, sympathetic qualities.

"I already said we'd adopted him." She looked up at me. "Well, we have. . .sort of," Jana said to my raised eyebrows.

"I don't think anyone is going to listen to Dicky Dunlap," I told her in an effort to contribute something positive to our mother/daughter discussion. In this rare opportunity for dialogue, I seized upon the chance to nurture Jana's confidence in Mom's point of view.

"They listen," Jana sighed. "He brags and they listen. Of course, it helps that he hit the most runs batted in for the Hawks two years in a row."

"Interesting," I mused out loud, "and I remember when he couldn't hit the toilet."

Jana snapped her head around and lay wide and disgusted eyes on me. "Mom! That's gross!"

I shrugged. "But true," I added with a grin back at her.

"When?" Jana demanded, keeping her voice harsh, but trying not to smile, I thought.

"Remember when he used to deliver the *Globe*?"

"That was years ago."

"Yeah, you were both in fifth grade, and he'd hang around waiting for you if you weren't home. One afternoon he managed to stall by asking to use the bathroom."

Jana giggled then. "I remember. You were mopping up the floor when I came in."

"So next time you see him, warn him to keep quiet about your business, or you and your mother will expose a nasty little secret that we've been keeping quiet about for years."

"What if he asks me what that secret is? I'd die before I told him."

"Be delicate about it. Tell him you came home to find your poor, hardworking mother bailing out the bathroom after the last time he used it."

"Oh, Mom!" Jana scoffed. But out of the corner of my eye I could see she was chuckling in spite of herself.

All the way home we had expected to run into the four-legged churchgoer, but Terrance had been nowhere in sight. Now, as we turned the corner of our street, we both stopped to assess the situation.

"Franny will be worried sick if she's discovered that Terrance has run away again," Jana lamented.

"He'll come home like he did last time," I said before I remembered that I was not exactly sure in my heart just how he had gotten home last time, never mind how he had run away in the first place.

I let out a whistle of sorts. It was so weak that it seemed to practically fall at my feet. "Can't begin to whistle like Franny." I shrugged at the pathetic expression with which Jana regarded me.

Then her face changed. It lit up. Her eyes widened, and her body tensed. "There he is," she almost whispered, looking over my shoulder and up the street we had just been on.

I turned to scan the sidewalk, expecting to see the marathon streak of white dog closing on us, but it was empty.

"Where?" I asked, turning back to Jana's same charged expression.

Then I heard the brassy echo of rock music as if it were coming from a cave; only I knew the cave would be moving, and the Disco King would be driving it.

He cruised up to us and turned the corner where we were standing like two moronic statues staring at him. It was the first time I'd been so close and gotten such a long look at the guy.

As he rounded the corner and passed us, he stared back, and in that instant, something familiar flickered in my memory and died in the same moment. Then he was drifting off, looking straight ahead again with the music wafting in waves of noise so loud they were almost visible.

Neither one of us moved until he was completely gone. Then Jana sighed, and I looked at her and hoped that the revulsion I felt was not recorded on my face.

"What in the name of common sense," I began, hearing the revulsion I had wished to visually conceal, "is the attraction?"

"Mom, the guy is so-o-o cool," Jana said in a tone that should have stopped further reproach on my part.

In my mind I saw the scene again as the Disco King floated by us covered with long dark hair and beard, his wreck of a car spewing an aura of thumping and churning noise, and I could only respond with a weak, "He is?"

"Yes, he is," she said in a voice that punctuated the end of the matter.

"But you can't even see his face," I pursued against the inner voice that was strongly advising me to back off.

"It's his eyes," she sighed, and then as an afterthought but important nonetheless, "and his very movements."

I was surprised to feel that flicker of familiarity sparkle and die a second time.

I shook off the disturbing sense of something so vague that it was easy to dodge and changed the subject. "This isn't finding Terrance," I said, and we both started walking toward the house again.

CHAPTER 8

There was no one at home, and that included Terrance. Both Jana and I agreed that Franny was undoubtedly out looking for the dog. I helped Jana throw a few last items into an overnight case, and while she got a beach bag together, I changed into a pair of shorts and a halter and got comfortable. Then I packed the brownies and potato salad that I had prepared the night before as contributions to Laurie's family reunion and sliced some cantaloupe and watermelon and added them to a small cooler. It was almost noon when I finished and called Jana's attention to the time. She appeared at the foot of the stairs with a bedroll and a teddy bear. I regarded her skeptically.

"Maybe the teddy bear should stay behind," I suggested.

"Laurie and I always have our teddy bears for overnights," she reminded me.

By the time the beach stuff, suitcase, and cooler were all together in the front hall, it was clear that Jana and her entourage would need to be taxied the short distance to Laurie's.

We packed the things into my tiny Celica Supra, and I drove up the street and around the block the long way so I'd be heading the short way toward the end of the court on my return home.

Laurie, who rushed out to meet us as we drove up, was clearly excited about the trip. When the paraphernalia had been transferred into the family's van, I hugged Jana good-bye.

"I hope you find Terrance," she said. Her genuine hug back reminded me of what a great hugger she had been right from the beginning, when the nurses would vie for the chance to hold her. They would tell me how she wrapped her little arms tight around their necks when they brought her in for a feeding. Now it struck me that she was a little hesitant about leaving despite the excitement of an overnight venture.

A blast of music interrupted our farewell. "Percy's playing 'Boogie-Oogie- Oogie,'" Jana laughed as we both jumped a bit at the sound.

"You be careful," I said, giving her one more hug.

"Oh, Mom," she said, dismissing my concern with a wave of a hand, "I'll be back tomorrow."

I had moved to open the car door when a piercing wail sounded from our street. "That blasted fruit and vegetable truck!" I said. "Such a noise, and on Sunday at that!"

I got in the car and started the engine.

"Who ever buys that stuff, anyway?" Jana asked. "It doesn't stop anywhere. It just drives around."

"See you tomorrow, Honey," I said to my daughter, and with one last wave I pulled the Supra out onto the court.

In the nick of time, I saw the hairy streak of dog come racing from around my back fence and straight into my path. I swerved to my right and deliberately across the lower part of the macho man's driveway, which was empty when I made the split-second decision. But a moment later, I crashed into the right rear side of his car, which had begun backing out just as I had swerved to avoid the dog.

I'd only been doing about five, maybe ten miles an hour, yet the front of my hood was crinkled, and steam was rising from it. Jana, screaming, with Laurie and then her parents, Dave and Louise, behind her, came racing the few feet to my door. Jana was the one who opened it.

"Are you okay, Mom?" her voice quivered as her arms reached in to help me as I shifted to swing my legs out of the car.

Terrance, his tongue hanging out and his beady little eyes gleaming, tried to jump in with me.

"I'm okay," I said quickly to erase the worry on my daughter's face. "Get that creature away from me!" I blurted. "Of all the stupid things! I should have run over the little bastard!"

"Mom!" Jana gasped at my language, and I looked sheepishly

first at her and then at Laurie's family, all regarding me with great concern and pity.

Dave went to inspect the front of my car and then the back of my neighbor's. The man I had always wanted to meet was getting out of his car now. I suddenly wished that I could disappear, but that would have been cowardly so I used the energy from my anger at the dog to launch myself from my own vehicle and stand on my own two feet. I was surprised, however, that I actually did feel shaky.

Just then Terrance noticed the neighbor approaching from his side of the wreckage, and with one long guttural snarl, took off toward him, hair standing straight up, and I imagined his teeth bared.

"Terrance!" I shouted, but Jana and Laurie managed to grab his collar before he could chew up the guy or his socks.

"What's gotten into Terrance?" Jana muttered rhetorically as she dragged the pathetic hound back toward Laurie's house.

"I'm terribly sorry," I started to say as the man and I met at the point of impact.

He seemed not to hear. "Look, I'm in a hurry," he said. "Would you back your car up just enough to free mine so I can assess the damage?"

"Sure," I nodded.

I don't know what I had expected. That he would have yelled? Cursed? Inquired for my health?

My hood looked like it was indelibly etched into a grotesque smile. My neighbor's fender was crushed into his rear tire.

I got back into the Supra and started the motor. It started as if nothing had happened. I shifted into reverse and eased up on the clutch ever so gently. With only a faint grating sound, I was separated from the macho man. *That was a short relationship*, I mused to myself as I shut off the engine and got back out. Jana and Laurie had taken Terrance over to the house to secure him in the dog run. Laurie's dad, Dave Burgess, and the man were peering at his bumper.

"You can't drive it this way, Nick," Dave was saying. "The bumper is impacting almost totally on the wheel."

I was standing at the scene of a two-car collision that had been completely my fault. (I'd hit the victim in his own driveway, for God's sake!) My car continued to steam and hiss and smile, and I had the unmitigated gall to feel elated at finally hearing the name of my macho neighbor!

Nick bent over, took hold of his twisted fender with his bare hands and pulled. The fender came forward a little at the two spots where his hands had been, but that indented the neighboring areas more.

"That's good enough for now," he announced, slapping his hands together and starting back around his car.

"I wouldn't drive it," Dave Burgess cautioned a second time.

"I've got no choice. I've got to get going," Nick stated matter-of-factly across the roof as he opened his car door. For a moment he and I locked eyes, and then he was in the car. The engine started, and the damaged vehicle began backing up with a ludicrous thumping sound as the fender and tire thwacked their way out of the court and disappeared around the corner of Grayson Street.

We all just stood for many seconds gaping at the empty court. "Dave," I finally broke the silence, "who is that guy?"

Dave chuckled as if to ward off his own amazement at what had just happened. "A nice enough fella," he shook his head and rubbed his hand across the back of his neck. "I don't really know much about him. His hours are different from mine, so we seldom get a chance to chat across the yard."

"Do you know what he does for a living?"

Dave began to smile. "Insurance adjuster, I should think," he teased. Then he became serious. "I really don't know, but he doesn't seem very concerned about the damage, does he?"

"I suppose, since we're neighbors, he figures he'll get the vital statistics later," I mused aloud. "Still, I need to have some information before I can put a claim in."

Just then a police car came into the court. Dale was driving.

"What happened?" he asked, looking at me and at my car and back at me. He had just braked in the middle of the court, put his flashing lights on and exited the cruiser, the motor still running. Afterwards, I would remember a lack of surprise on Dale's part, as if he always rode around the court and found accidents. It was the lack of the double-take, the sense I had that he had already known that he would stop just around my fence and there we'd be.

"I had an accident," I told him.

"Who hit you?" Dale was studying my grimacing car front and peering at the tire marks my car had made.

"I hit my neighbor's car broadside," I said.

"And it disappeared?" he asked, looking around dramatically.

"He had to go," I said lamely.

"So he had no damage?" Dale had taken a small notebook out of his shirt pocket and was making a couple of notes in regard, I thought, to the tire marks he was looking at again.

"Nick really shouldn't have driven the car," Dave Burgess spoke up. "It has a seriously damaged right bumper."

Dale nodded his curly head and kept writing.

"Nick Who?" he asked me.

I shrugged, raising my hands, palms up.

"You didn't swap papers?" Dale asked, lowering his notebook then to stare at me.

"There was no time. The guy just. . .left." I shrugged again and dropped my palms.

"Nick Michaels," Dave Burgess volunteered.

My heart took another extra beat as I recorded the fact that the macho man had a last name. Then I remembered it was I who had just forced the man with both a first and last name to drive away with an embarrassing lisp resounding from his rear bumper.

"Think you can drive this car to your garage?" Dale was asking. A crowd had started to gather. I even saw Martha at the edge of her lawn squinting into the sun as she eyed the commotion.

Then Jana, who had returned from dog duty, put her left hand in almost a salute position across her forehead and groaned. I looked over the crowd and, sure enough, there was Dicky Dunlap pushing his way toward me.

"Gee, Mrs. Connors," he said as he approached, "is this your car?"

"What's left of it, Dicky," I sighed.

"Look," I said to Dave, "why don't you get started. You're behind schedule now. Dale can help me get my wreck home."

"Mom, are you sure you're okay to stay alone tonight?" Jana asked, her face full of genuine concern.

I cupped her cheeks with my hands, and for the first time since she'd turned thirteen, I had my little girl back.

"Honey, I was only going five miles an hour, and I'm fine. Besides," I added, "Franny only works until midnight on Sundays so she'll be home earlier than usual. You go have a good time."

Jana gave me another lingering hug. "You be careful," she said, echoing my own concern to her earlier.

I had everything I could do to keep the tears from showing. *Somehow it all comes around,* I remember thinking. *Once the adolescent demons get resolved, she'll be my best support. I must be more careful because she's picking up on my examples of caring and concern.*

"God, Mrs. Connors, what a mess!" It was Dicky Dunlap, who had reached my grinning hood. I wanted to throttle him. Just when I had Jana on her way toward the van with Laurie, he had to remind her of the damage she was leaving. I saw her hesitate and look back at us.

I shook hands with Dave and gave Louise a hug. "Have a good time," I told them. I could hear Dale behind me cautioning Dicky Dunlap not to push on my hood.

Finally, the Burgess van was off with energetic waves.

"Send me a postcard," Dicky yelled at Jana, evidently convinced that the outing was one of duration. I chuckled as I watched Jana assume the Dicky Dunlap salute. We all kind of froze where we were until the van had turned out of the court and out of sight.

"Let's get you home," Dale said.

I climbed into my car and started the motor. Dale backed his cruiser up into Nick Michaels's driveway, lights still flashing, and escorted me the short distance around my fence and out into Grayson Street, where I turned left into my driveway.

Dale offered to contact a body shop for me, and would have stayed to help further, I was sure, but I lied and said I was tired and would deal with it in the morning. I was struck again with the importance of distancing myself from him even though truthfully I could have used some good advice about the next step in my dilemma.

As it turned out, Joey called soon after Dale had left and was immediately concerned about the accident, so much so that he arranged for his company's garage to come after my car the next morning. And he insisted that I use one of his classic automobiles, which he collected as a hobby, while I waited for my Supra to be fixed.

Franny came in while I was on the phone with Joey. When I hung up, I found her upstairs getting ready to go to work.

"Did you see my car?" I asked her. When she gave me a puzzled look, I told her what had happened.

"Here I have the chance of a lifetime to squash Terrance like the insect he is, and I do the honorable thing and hit my neighbor's car instead," I ranted. "By the way, your friend is strange."

"What friend?" she paused to look at me in the middle of zipping up her dress.

"Nick Michaels," I said, pronouncing his name syllable by syllable to assure clarity.

"Don't know him," she said and went back to dressing.

In frustration, I turned on my heels and left Franny and her lies.

CHAPTER 9

Franny didn't even say good-bye. I heard her talking to Terrance in the dog run as she fed him, and then her car started up out front and she was gone. I looked around at the suddenly empty and quiet afternoon. The stillness of it hung heavy in front of me and filled my ears with its vacuum. It seemed strange to be without Jana somewhere close by, and the growing tension between Franny and me gnawed at my already shaky sense of well-being.

I brought Terrance in when the day turned to dusk around eight-fifteen. I had spent what had been left of the afternoon reading and pampering myself. Just before eight, I had poured myself a Dubonnet and sat with it on the front steps.

Nick Michaels had not returned home yet, and if I had intended to collect the necessary data sometime during the afternoon, I wouldn't have been able to. The fact that I didn't even know Nick's number plate would have worried me except that there were plenty of witnesses, and the accident had been completely my fault. Since this was Sunday, I would wait and notify the insurance company first thing tomorrow. Nick Michaels surely would be home between now and nine A.M.

The Dubonnet tasted every bit as good as it had on Friday night, the day Franny had moved in. Had it only been two days since she'd arrived? How could so much have happened in so short a time? It seemed as though Franny had brought one mishap after another with her. Still, she was my friend, and if we could part on good terms, that was what I hoped for. It was with this thought that I got up, took another sip of my wine, and went around the right side of the house and through the gate to the dog run. Being sure to latch the gate behind me, I released Terrance and led him wriggling and wagging expectantly around the swimming pool and up the stairs to the back deck slider.

"Don't take this personally," I cautioned him as I opened the door. "I like your mother, that's all."

The dog hit the dining room carpet and immediately pranced toward his favorite spot in the living room. I turned to close the slider screen in time to see Nick Michaels sauntering up his porch steps with a woman behind him. The car in his driveway was not familiar to me. "He must have ditched the wreck," I mumbled as I retrieved my wine and took one last sip.

"No time like the present," I mused and rummaged through my catch-all kitchen drawer for a tiny notebook I knew was there. Finding it and grabbing a pen from the counter, I let myself out the front door and walked around the left side of my Colonial and up the court, past Martha's, to the green house at the bend.

It was a beautiful and warm night, just barely light now, but Nick's inside door was closed against the screen, which would have provided lovely evening breezes from the southeast.

The wine had made me sleepy, and I pictured myself slumbering soon with the help of the wine and the June breezes that always came through my front bedroom windows.

I was surprised to find Nick's screen door locked and no doorbell, so I knocked as best I could on the steel strip that ran along the sides of the screening. Nothing happened.

I tried knocking on the lower, all-steel section, and waited again. Nothing.

They haven't had time to get into a compromising position, I thought, and then the inside door opened.

The woman said, "Yes?"

Where had I seen her face before? "I'd like to see Nick Michaels," I told her. "I won't take long."

"Nobody here by that name," she said and started to close the door.

"But he lives here," I managed to blurt out before the door slammed shut.

Flabbergasted, I stood staring at the closed door feeling surprise, anger, and then alarm, in that order. I thought about pounding on the screen until Nick came and talked to me, but the picture of Franny at the boarded-up houses last night made me turn and walk slowly across the porch and down the steps.

If Laurie's folks had been home, I would have gone next door and asked their advice. If the woman had said Nick was busy, or unable to come to the door, I might have felt better about the encounter, but what a strange thing to say. Did Nick really think I wouldn't at least know his name? And why was he avoiding me, anyway? I was trying to follow legal protocol, after all.

I needed Nick Michaels's information by nine tomorrow morning. I thought of calling Dale at home and thought better of it instantly. I wasn't sure Dale was living at home on any given day, and if he wasn't, I didn't want to bother Susan, his long-suffering wife.

By the time I'd rounded the corner and reached my door, I had decided on an acceptable alternative strategy.

Terrance growled as I entered the house but began wagging his whole body when he recognized me. "How can you look so happy to see someone who hates you so much?" I asked on my way to the phone in the kitchen. He wiggled even harder at the sound of my voice.

I dialed the police as I made a mental note of two facts: I'd never called the police before Franny had moved in, and this was the second call to them from this house in forty-eight hours.

When the officer at the desk answered, I identified myself and asked if I could leave a message for Dale Mercer. "What time will he be in in the morning?" I asked, figuring that he must be on the day shift this week, based upon his midday appearance at the accident scene.

"Sorry," the officer told me, "Dale's been on vacation all week. He has one more to go."

"But he handled a traffic matter for me just today," I protested, bewildered for a second time within a half hour.

"Not officially," came the response. "You want another officer?"

I said I'd think about it and hung up. I was shaking. What did it all mean? What was going on?

First, my neighbor. Didn't he want to put a claim in on his car just as much as I did? Even more so because he'd been the innocent party? Maybe the woman was his girlfriend and thought I was after her man. But I'd never seen him with her before, and if she'd been jealous she had not looked resentful or angry a few minutes ago, just totally aloof.

Her face at the door replayed in my mind. What was it about her face? She seemed too old for him, or was that just sour grapes like my not being impressed by any of the ladies I'd seen going in and out of the house with him this past year?

And what was going on with Dale? He'd been on vacation for a week? How could that be? He was in uniform, in a city patrol car when he came upon the accident this morning.

Then I remembered how quickly and conveniently he'd arrived in the court. As if it had all been prearranged, which of course it had not been. Nothing involving Terrance could ever be anything but unpredictable—unless, of course, someone decided to prearrange his death, which I'd been tempted to do many times. Twice so far on this day alone!

I managed to congratulate myself for a semblance of humor even after all this chaos. My mind sped from the unfathomable meeting with the lady in the green house, only to race back to the equally unfathomable telephone call just now to the police department.

Was this what it felt like to lose one's mind? Living bits and pieces of experiences that didn't fit together into a logical cause-and-effect pattern?

I knew that in my present state I shouldn't do it, but I poured another Dubonnet into the empty glass I'd left on the counter. The phone rang as I was pouring it. The sudden intrusive sound almost made me drop the bottle. I took a good sip before I answered on the third ring.

"Hi," he said in his familiar cheery tone, "just checking in to see how you're doing after this morning's catastrophe."

"Dale?" I gasped.

"You okay, Janet?" came the reply. "You sound," a pause,

"strung out, as they say."

"Dale," I said again, trying to keep my voice level and without emotion, "I called the station a few minutes ago to leave you a message, and the desk sergeant said you'd been on vacation for a week."

Dale's easy laugh surprised me. "Must be old Nesbit on the desk," he chuckled. "He can never read the schedule correctly. My vacation starts the end of the week. I'll be off for two weeks, and I earned it." Another good-natured laugh. "I hope you called me for a date."

"No chance," I said, and then let a bit of my concern invade my voice as I told him about the bizarre encounter at Nick Michaels's house a short time before.

"I'll see what I can do, Honey," Dale assured me. "He can't withhold that kind of information. I'll see you have it by the time the insurance companies open tomorrow."

I must admit I was much relieved when I hung up the phone moments later. Dale had seemed like his old relaxed self as he fended off my doubts and calmed my uneasiness. If the fact that he had called me so soon after my call to the station seemed too coincidental, I chose to slide any further suspicion into the back of my mind.

I finished my Dubonnet, melted a slice of cheese over a dropped egg on a piece of toasted wheat bread, and went to bed about nine o'clock. I did take several minutes to barricade Terrance in the kitchen by placing a bench and a chair at the doorway to the dining room and a card table and a chair at the other doorway into the foyer. He looked at me forlornly as I waved a casual good night from the hall stairs.

Just as I had hoped, the breeze and the wine, not to mention the stress of the day's events, all worked in unison to bring on a deep sleep with great rapidity.

I was, therefore, distraught to find myself summoned up from this totally peaceful respite by Terrance's barking. I groaned and turned to look at the clock. Eleven! Could Terrance be barking because of Franny's arrival? I couldn't believe he'd bark at Franny. I couldn't believe that Franny was home at eleven.

I could hear the dog leaping against the card table with such force that it was audibly rocking the chair that braced it.

I rolled over and swung my legs off the bed.

I rubbed my eyes and checked the clock radio again to be sure I'd been right about the time. I had been. It was now a minute after eleven.

I put my feet on the floor and prepared myself to put weight on them. I was facing the hallway outside my open bedroom door. The glow from the burglar-alarm box in the center of the upstairs hallway lit up the area outside my room, but something else in the shimmering eeriness of its spidery rays made me freeze on the edge of the bed. A shadow that was never among the regular dark waves in the hallway's illumination was etched against the otherwise normal patterns. Stunned, I watched paralyzed as a darkened form moved away from my bedroom door.

The previous owners had installed the alarm system, which had to be manually triggered by a single switch at the main entrance in the foyer. It was a truly ineffective contraption that would never alert the homeowner to a burglar unless the burglar accidentally bumped against the wall button on his way in or out of the front door. Then red lights would flash on the roof and sirens would wail in the house, but no connection had ever been made into the local police department. Needless to say, the whole device had always gone unnoticed. Until now!

Now I continued to stare into its kaleidoscopic patterns in search of... what? An intruder?

I tried to scold myself into thinking it must be Franny. Who else had a key? Who else would be up on the second floor? *Franny is home early*, I told myself. But I hesitated to call her name, and Terrance kept up his frenzied barking and lunging at the makeshift barricade. Certainly, if Franny had come home, she would not have tolerated his discomfort nor his confinement for a moment.

The sharp pain of this reality struck a new terror in my gut and brought me to my feet. The bed squeaked as I released my weight from it, and I stood still, holding my breath, my eyes wide and searching the corridor wall for another unfamiliar etching.

There wasn't one, and so slowly, step by step, I inched my

way toward the bedroom door, keeping myself in the shadows to the left of its opening. Jana's words echoed in my head: "Are you sure you're okay to stay alone tonight?" I was glad, if this were an intruder, that she was safely away.

Without exposing myself, I peered around the edge of the door just enough to study the total hallway. If anyone were lurking there, his shadow would give him away. The pattern had returned to the normal fluttery zigs and zags emanating from beady red and green eyes on the alarm box.

Suddenly, there was a terrific crash, and just as I would have dived for cover, I realized that the noise had come from downstairs as Terrance finally toppled the card table enough to leap into the foyer. I could hear him snarling and pattering up the stairs.

He didn't come into my room. He didn't even slow down at my door. I peeked around in time to see him reach the top of the landing and lunge down the corridor toward Franny's room.

I took the opportunity to dart around the doorway and fling myself two or three steps at a time to the main floor, release the bolt on the outside door, and run out onto the front walk. Franny's car was not in the driveway. She was not home yet. The shadow had not been hers.

Somehow being in the open space made me feel better, but not for long. I was in a pair of flimsy baby-doll pajamas. It was after eleven o'clock. The Burgesses were out of town. Where could I go to call the police? I hadn't dared to stay in the house to do it. I decided Martha's was the nearest place and headed across the lawn toward the edge of the court. If Martha didn't respond to my knock, I could see lights still glowing at Mrs. Murphy's, across from Martha's in the old-age home.

I was so intent on my destination and on forming alternative plans of refuge that I didn't hear any movement before I was grabbed from behind. His arm came out to lift me around the waist and off my feet as his other hand simultaneously clamped itself firmly against my mouth.

In seconds, he had dragged me back behind the azaleas that grew thick and tall at the side of my house at the base of the wide chimney. I was flailing my legs and trying to open my mouth to scream or bite his offending hand, but I was no match for his strength.

Once behind the bushes, I waited wide-eyed with terror to be raped or assaulted in some way. My heart was trying to pound its way out of my chest. At first I tried prying at the hand around my waist to no avail, and so I began clawing at the arm. Somehow, he managed to juggle me and pin both of my arms under his one arm that held me, rendering me even more helpless.

I don't know when I began realizing that he had been whispering in my ear the whole time. "It's all right, I'm not here to hurt you. You're safe. We just need to stay here a few minutes. I won't harm you."

His rhetoric didn't serve to calm me, not with his vise-like grip around my upper body and his hand secured tightly over my mouth. I forced myself to assess as much as I could about him under the circumstances. One of my hands could still reach one of his arms and hands, and I felt a watch with an expansion band and a large ring with a high smooth stone. My left index finger began inspecting that ring. I could make out a rough oval setting with a raised gem. A class ring perhaps.

I continued to flail my legs, and tried to scream, but could only emit squeaky, worthless sounds because of his muzzling hand. We were locked together like this for what seemed an interminably long time. There was no way to get a glimpse of my attacker, and the shrubs hid any view of us from the court or Grayson Street.

There wasn't a sound except for the constant whispers of the man who held me captive. I hadn't heard Terrance since I'd bolted out the door. No cars went by while we played out this horrifying scene in the damp, dark abyss behind the azaleas.

Then I heard, ever so softly, a dull whistle in back of my house and suddenly I was released and the man was gone.

I'd been thrown off balance when he let me go, and by the time it sank in that my assailant had fled, I was stumbling out of the bushes. There was no sign of anyone, nor did I hear anything after that almost imperceptible whistle, which could, I thought, have come from the court near Laurie's house.

I stepped back and stayed still like a dolt, slightly behind the azaleas. I wasn't about to chase my attacker, if you could call him that, and I hesitated to come out of the shadows to be a target for whoever else might still be around. So I stood and listened. I guess I wondered if I'd hear a car engine or running feet or hushed voices, but I continued to hear nothing, and so eventually I took the final step out onto the lawn and looked back at the house. All seemed normal. Inching my way toward the front door, but constantly glancing around, I managed to ascertain that the door was still open, though the screen door had automatically shut after me, as usual.

As I debated my next move, Franny drove into the driveway. I'd heard a car turn into Grayson and had braced myself to make a run back to the shadows or to Martha's.

Franny was by my side almost the moment she got the car stopped. Seeing me on the front lawn in nightwear close to midnight was a clue that something was very wrong.

"Franny!" I blurted, and then I started to cry. I never cry, but I was suddenly shaking from head to foot, and once the tears started, there was no way to stop the sobs that followed.

Franny had her arms wrapped around me instantly and began edging us toward the front steps.

"We can't go in there," I croaked through my sobs.

"What's happened?" she asked. She was so calm; so in control.

"There was a prowler. . .upstairs," I choked out. "If it hadn't been for Terrance. . . ," I said, looking at Franny. I knew I was wild-eyed and staring dully at her like a lunatic.

I stepped back so I could grab both her shoulders. "Call Terrance, Franny," I commanded. "See if he's all right."

Franny didn't let go of me and by nudges, encouraged me to mount the front steps.

"Just whistle or call him through the screen," I said through the tension in my voice.

Franny let go of me and let out one of her whistle-like-a-man whistles, which required both of her index fingers. I remembered how Terrance had responded like a boomerang the last time she'd done that. This time we waited and nothing happened.

"Oh, God!" I wailed. "He's dead! They've killed him!"

"Nonsense," Franny said. "Who'd want to kill Terrance?"

"I did," I sobbed, "and he loved me and rushed to my defense, and it's like I have killed him myself! Poor Terrance!" I pictured him wagging his whole body expectantly when I'd let him in tonight; so trusting. And now he was dead, and I might as well have rendered the fatal blow personally.

"Let's go in to see about Terrance," Franny coaxed.

"I. . .we can't go in there, Franny. We need the police."

"I thought we should never call the police," Franny reminded me.

"This time we need to," I said. "I can't go back in there unless the police go in first."

"*I'll* go in first," Franny said.

"Franny," I was beginning to get a grip on myself again. "I was accosted by a man there in the bushes not five minutes ago. And this was after someone got into the house."

"How do you know?" Franny interrupted.

"Franny, the guy grabbed me right over there," I pointed to the middle of the lawn.

"I mean how do you know someone got into the house?"

"I saw him—or rather, his shadow—up in the second floor hallway. Then Terrance broke loose from his barricade, and—"

"What barricade?" Franny interrupted again.

"I set up a flimsy barricade to keep Terrance in the kitchen tonight. I figured since you and he wouldn't be here much longer, I'd start now to cut down on living room hair follicles, but he jumped through and ran upstairs, which gave me time to run downstairs and out the door."

"Probably looking for me," Franny said calmly, opening the screen and entering the foyer.

"Franny, it wasn't like that!" I protested in alarm. I was outside the screen door talking in to her. "The dog was growling and snarling. He knew someone was upstairs."

"He doesn't like to be confined," I heard Franny say as she picked up the card table and carried the chair back to the kitchen.

I flung both hands up over my head and did a semi-pivot

right there on the front stoop.

Then I got mad. "Look, Franny," I said, yanking the door open and storming through the foyer and into the kitchen, where Franny was calmly dismantling the other barricade next to the dining room, "I woke up to Terrance's snarls and growls and saw someone in the upstairs hall."

Franny slid the bench back behind one side of the dining room table. "But you didn't actually see him," she said, pausing to look at me.

"I saw his shadow, and then I was able to get down the stairs and out the door because Terrance was so distraught that he'd been able to knock down the card table and go upstairs after. . ." I stopped short. "Franny, why aren't you looking for Terrance?" I demanded.

Franny was pouring Dubonnet into a goblet. "Here," she said handing it to me, "you need this. Take a few sips and calm down. I'll go look for Terrance if you sit here," she gestured at a chair at the kitchen table.

I looked suspiciously at her. "Franny, why are you so unbelievably calm? Terrance may be dead upstairs and you're so calm."

"I'll go look," was all she said.

I sat down and took a sip, then two more. My eyes fell on the steel cellar door. It was closed like I had left it. Was it also bolted like I'd left it?

I got up and walked over to the door. The bolt was in place. If someone had been upstairs, they must have gone out the front door while I was being detained behind the bushes, or. . . My eyes lifted toward the ceiling. "Franny!" I wailed, shoving my drink onto the kitchen table and hurrying to the foot of the stairs.

Franny was coming down them as I put my foot hesitantly on the first step.

"Terrance is not up there," Franny said, still very calm. "He must have come right out of the door behind you when you ran out."

"He didn't," I said.

"Did you actually hear him barking from upstairs when you got outside?" she asked.

I had to say that I had not. "But I saw him turn and lunge down the hall toward your room just as I ran down to the front door," I said.

"You were so distraught by that time that you just didn't notice him behind you."

"He would have barked when the man grabbed me if he'd been out there with me."

"This man," Franny said slowly, "what did he look like?"

"I never saw him. He grabbed me from behind."

"And you think he was the prowler?"

"I didn't think so at the time; I don't know if the prowler could have come out of the house behind me. . ." My voice tapered off as I contemplated that possibility.

"Janet," Franny began. We were in the kitchen again and she was wiping up the Dubonnet I had spilled in my rush to check on her. She handed me the glass. "Janet," she said again, "you're telling me that you might have missed a full-grown man following you out of the house, but you know a little dog wasn't behind you?"

"Franny, once that screen closed, Terrance couldn't open it, and I know the dog was not right behind me. Of course," a new thought, "Terrance could have come out on the heels of the prowler. . .

"No," I said, immediately changing my mind before Franny had a chance to respond, "I'd have heard him growling and snarling in that case. I'd have been tipped off that the man was behind me. No, the prowler and my assailant were two different men and Terrance wasn't with either of them."

Franny sighed and sat down at the table. "Janet, I think there was no prowler; that Terrance was just upset at being closed in, and when you went downstairs he followed right out the door."

I shook my head. "It just didn't happen like that. And you certainly can't explain away my attacker."

"Show me your bruises."

"He didn't hurt me."

"Well, he wasn't interested in picking your pockets," she smirked.

I looked down at my scanty attire. I didn't like what she was suggesting.

"He wasn't a pervert, either," I countered.

"Sounds like you're defending him," she chuckled. "He didn't hurt you; he didn't get fresh; what exactly *did* he do?"

"Just. . .just detained me for maybe three minutes, and then he was gone. It was as if he was waiting for something. And I think I heard a faint whistle just before he disappeared."

"Disappeared," Franny scoffed, "as in a puff of smoke?"

"Franny, why are you acting this way? You could see I was distraught when you pulled up."

"Of course I could," she said, rising slowly from the chair and reaching for my drink. As she clinked three cubes into the glass, she gave me a concerned look.

"I've got to call the police before another minute goes by," I said, reaching for the phone over my head.

"My point exactly," Franny said. "Call the police and tell them what you just told me? They'll ask you the same questions I did, and your answers will sound. . .well. . .disoriented."

"Franny, I'm no wacko. I've got to report what happened to me tonight."

"Well," she said, pausing to think, "I guess you could mention that Terrance is missing again, after all, his disappearance is part of your story."

"Yes, it is," I said, suddenly convinced that Franny had mentioned Terrance only to dissuade me from calling the police and reliving the circus of three nights ago. Well, if that was her intent, it hadn't worked. I punched in 9 and the first 1 before she grabbed the receiver.

"All right," Franny said, clicking off the connection and then dialing again. "I know the guy on duty after midnight." She winked at me. "He just left me at eleven," she whispered over the mouthpiece she was covering with her hands.

I nodded with a twisted mouth that told her my opinion of a cop who reports for his night shift from a bar down the street.

"He wasn't drinking," she said in an offended tone. "We were just getting better acquainted. I'll tell him what happened. It's an excuse to call him."

"They tape those conversations, don't forget."

She chose to ignore my remark, and I must say did an excellent job recapping my story. She explained how distraught I was and how she wished to spare me the trouble of rehashing the whole thing, and then she reiterated, in remarkable chronology, the events of the night as they had happened to me.

When she had finished, she listened briefly, then said, "Oh, I'll tell her. That must be it."

Another pause and a smile crawled across her face. "Oh, I will," she sighed with a hicuppy giggle and hung up.

"You did fine, Franny. Thank you. What did he say?"

"He said that they've been alerted to an area Peeping Tom in the last two weeks."

Again I shook my head in disagreement. "Peeping Toms don't grab women or break into houses."

"No, but you don't really know that anyone broke in. How would he have gotten in?"

I looked at the cellar door, which I knew had remained bolted. That left the front door and the deck slider, both of which I knew had definitely been bolted also. "I don't know," I said, rubbing my forehead. "How did someone get in the other time?"

Franny looked at me with what seemed to me to be concern that bordered on the obsequious. "Maybe no one did," she said quietly. "Maybe Terrance got out when you opened the door that time, as well."

"Oh, I don't know, Franny." I stopped cold. "Franny," I said, "you never mentioned to your friend at the station that Terrance was missing."

"He'll come back," she said, standing up and stretching wearily. "He always does. I'm going to bed."

"You are?" I gasped. "You mean no searches this time? No posters? No pounding on neighborhood doors?" I was dumbfounded, picturing a hysterical Franny the last time Terrance had disappeared. I saw her sobbing, flashing accusing looks and muttering hurtful retorts, calling the police, taking time off from work, and, in general, making a great spectacle of herself!

"You're going to bed? You actually can sleep?" I continued incredulously as I followed her through the foyer. She was yawning loudly as she climbed the stairs.

"Good night, Janet," she said, without looking back at me.

I watched her ascent with my mouth hanging open in disbelief. Finally I checked that the front door was locked and extinguished the kitchen lights. Then, with leaden steps, I followed the flickering glow of the infamous alarm box to the second floor.

I showered vigorously and changed into clean pajamas. It was much later, however, before I collapsed into bed. And I did not sleep until the light began to show along the edges of my window curtains.

CHAPTER 10

I didn't sleep much once dawn arrived, either. I just fell into irritating pits with troubled images that I couldn't recall whenever I came up to wakefulness.

I finally forced myself out of bed at six-thirty.

I put on a robe and walked through the upstairs rooms before I went downstairs. I don't know what I expected to find in the light of day, but all was in order. I did not risk waking Franny, who slept behind her closed door as I moved quietly by it.

I needed coffee. I knew, upon finally waking, that I had to do some serious thinking.

Last night, from upset and weariness, I had let myself begin to doubt the presence of an intruder. This morning, my belief in the prowler was renewed.

It had not escaped my notice that Franny had chosen to downplay, or just plain ignore, my abduction into the bushes, choosing instead to concentrate on shooting holes in my story of an intruder inside the house.

And then there was her sudden change of attitude. Last night, I had been too tired to deal with her aloofness concerning Terrance's disappearance. Today, hopefully, I could look at all the aspects of last night with a clearer head.

The percolator soon spewed wonderful aromas across the kitchen and out into the other areas of the first floor, and somehow that allowed me to take possession of my home and comfort from it once again.

I wandered around the first floor remembering the night before, but my thoughts kept tumbling into each other. I felt restless, chaotic. The coffee was taking forever to perk.

At seven I showered again, and while I roughly fluffed my wet hair, I slipped into a halter and shorts, poured my first cup of coffee, and took it out onto the front steps.

"I should be walking," I addressed my mug before I took a sip from it. But my body still wanted to rest, and walking would have been pushing myself. No fun doing that.

I swallowed the hot coffee and studied the street. It would be a sizzler today. Already the air conditioners buzzed in half of the apartments at the old-age home.

"Mornin', Kiddo," Happy greeted as he jogged by. Heat or no heat, he was doing his daily workout.

"I should be walking," I mumbled into my cup again.

I took my coffee and walked across the lawn to the corner of the house to look behind the azaleas. I guess I thought some clue of my abduction might be visible in the daylight.

It wasn't.

There was no sign of a struggle there. Mostly, I'd been lifted off the ground. Whoever had held me had not left *his* tracks, either.

What did I know about the man who had grabbed me? He was tall. He had thick hair on his arms, but I could not say if he was blond or brunette. He wore a watch and a ring and a fragrance. Suddenly I was recalling a smell. Was it aftershave? Did the Peeping Tom wear cologne? Why did that seem incongruous to me?

What bothered me most about my attacker was his purpose. I really didn't buy the Peeping-Tom scenario. So what was he doing lurking around my house, and why did he grab me only to let me go a few minutes later? His constant assurances that I wouldn't be hurt had evidently been the truth. "My gentleman attacker," I murmured and took another sip of coffee.

Wearily, I walked back to the steps and sat down once more. Mr. Peddington from the perfect house on the corner started his lawn sprinklers. Mrs. Murphy set a bowl outside her apartment door at the old-age home for any animals that might need sustenance during the day. She didn't have any pets herself, but she always kept something for the neighborhood cats and dogs. Today, because of the heat, I was sure it would be liquid.

I heard the footsteps to my right before he came into view along the court's sidewalk. When he did appear, he was dressed as he had been Friday night—impeccably pressed pants and a crisp shirt, its collar slightly up. As he turned the corner toward me, I saw the top two buttons characteristically undone.

Self-consciously, I straightened the wet towel around my shoulders and tried to fluff my hair, which was still damp and, I hoped, springy around my face. Of all the times I'd wanted my macho neighbor to notice me, here he finally was at my door, and here I was, exhausted from lack of sleep, totally without makeup, and a bit soggy to boot.

"Good morning," he said as he started up my short, red-brick walk. "I've brought the information you'll be needing today."

When he reached me, he put one shiny loafered foot on the second step for balance as he dug into his back pocket.

Out came a folded piece of white paper, and I had time to watch a dark strand of hair fall across his forehead as he opened his notes and studied them briefly. When he looked up, I stumbled into the softest brown eyes that I had ever seen in a man.

"This is all the data you should need," he said, looking back at the paper. "This is my license plate, insurance company, address, phone number." He was stabbing each item with his left hand, which wore a signet ring below the arm that wore a watch with an expansion band! I caught my breath and stared at the arm and not the paper.

"What kind of ring is that?" I blurted in a voice that was nothing more than a squawk. "Graduation?"

"Maritime Academy," he said, "1962 commencement."

For a moment our eyes locked, and then he shifted his vision back to the paper, and refolding it, handed it to me.

"I won't be home at all today," he said. "If you need any further information, you can call me tonight. I'm hoping to go on vacation tomorrow. I'll get any information I need from you before I leave."

His foot came off the step with a light scraping sound as he shifted to go.

"Your cologne is familiar. What is it?" I said to his back. I heard the defiance in my voice as I spoke the words that I had not consciously commanded myself to say.

He squared his shoulders ever so imperceptibly before he turned and looked at me.

The warm eyes reflected a new emotion. Why did I think it was, regret?

"Brut," he said, keeping his gaze fixed on mine for a moment. Then he left, walking back around the corner toward his house. I watched his every step until he was out of sight, willing him to look back at me, to return, to explain what he'd been doing in the shadows outside my house last night. But of course he only kept walking.

To try to describe what I was feeling as I sat there alone for the next half hour would be extremely difficult. So many emotions were crashing through me, I couldn't begin to reconcile any of them. I knew that I should begin to figure out some explanations for all the events of the three preceding days. An inner voice urged me to go in and pick up the phone and call the police now that I was sure of my attacker's identity.

Distorting this rational idea were conflicting images: Franny talking to my assailant and denying later that she knew him; Franny sobbing hysterically over the disappearance of her dog three days ago and going up to bed with a shrug last night when he turned up missing again. And Dale! On vacation or not? And was there a prowler last night and three nights ago? And if so, how were they managing to get into my house?

Throughout the ordeal of juggling these questions was the picture of warm brown eyes that I couldn't keep from my mind. And more questions. Had I misread the warmth of those dark eyes because I wanted to?

"Brut." His response kept ringing in my ears. The tone he'd used to say that one significant syllable had been full of disgust—or was I imagining that, too?

"I'm off," Franny burst through the front door with this brief announcement, and I jumped at least an inch.

"Off where?" I asked as she skirted me and went down the steps toward her car.

"Errands," she said cryptically, "and I'll probably go right to work tonight just as I am."

I noticed she was all dressed up. "It's only eight o'clock," I noted.

"Well, I got home at a decent hour last night," she said, tossing her pocketbook into the front seat and sliding slowly in behind the wheel.

"Franny," I said, putting my cup down and going over to lean on the driver's-side door.

Franny rolled her window down with a trace of reluctance, I thought.

She looked up at me after she'd turned the key and gotten the motor started. "You're still nervous about last night," she said.

I looked straight into her eyes as I nodded, "Even more so since I found out who grabbed me." I was leaning on her door with both hands, my elbows stiff, my shoulders hunched into my neck.

The look she gave me was a mixture of disbelief, curiosity, and fear. I knew she wanted to ask *who* because of emotions number one and two, but was hesitant to do so because of number three. I saved her the trouble of asking.

"Nick Michaels hauled me into the bushes last night," I stated. "I recognized his watchband and graduation ring."

"How would you possibly see those small items in the dark?" Franny scoffed as she shifted gears.

"I felt them," I said.

Franny shook her head firmly.

"Half a million men in New England wear watches and graduation rings," she began.

"See you later, Franny," I sighed, stepping back from the car. "I wish we were still the friends we used to be. Remember how you used to recite 'Jabberwocky' by heart every time I was feeling down? I could really use a verse or two about now!"

I flung these final words after her as she was backing the car out of the drive.

I watched her exit Grayson Street in a hurry, obviously relieved to get away from me. But why? How was Franny mixed up with this?

What *was* this?

I didn't have time for further contemplation because a four-door aberration of gray metal turned into the street and pulled up to the curb in front of my walk just as Franny disappeared from view. Joey was driving.

"I want to know what you call your pet dinosaur," I asked as he shut off the motor and grinned from ear to ear. I was conscious of looking a gift of extinction in the mouth, but there were no hard feelings because he gave me that wonderful gunshot laugh of his and opened the squeaky, albeit squeaky-clean, door. As he got out, a rumble of sound drew our attention back to the street as a tow truck pulled up behind Joey's antique.

"This the wreck you want hauled out of here, Mr. Lambert?" the hulk inside the truck said, gesturing toward the classic automobile whose chrome Joey had already begun polishing with a clean white handkerchief.

It was my turn to laugh, and this time, Joey gave me a look of irritation before he began directing the tow truck around and into the driveway. It took less than five minutes for Joey's mechanic to hook on to the front of my car and pull its shattered form out of the garage and onto the street to begin its journey of reconstruction.

"Hank's a good guy," Joey said as he turned to regard what must have seemed like a look of distress on my face as I stood watching the snakelike dance of truck and Toyota disappear around the corner. "He'll do a good job for you."

"I'm sure of it," I nodded, giving Joey a pat on the arm. "Want some coffee?"

"I'd love some," he beamed, and for the next half hour or so we sat side by side on the top step sipping coffee and watching the rest of the hot summer morning come alive. Peddington turned off his sprinklers and puttered in his yard. Mrs. Murphy shook some scatter rugs and checked the pet bowl. Martha waddled down her steps to toss some breakfast scraps onto the lawn under her clothesline for the birds to devour as soon as she went back inside. More air conditioners in the old-age complex were activated against the oppressive heat that, by eight-thirty, had wrapped Grayson Street in a cloak of gray haze.

Joey stood and stretched and handed me his empty cup. "Gotta go," he announced. "This heat is brutal already. How about dinner tonight?"

"Terrific," I said, "but it's on me. How about coming over at seven for a swim and some fried chicken and potato salad?"

"I could handle that," he grinned.

I watched him cut through the center courtyard of the housing complex. He'd work in his air-conditioned suite of offices over the bank up on Harley Street for the rest of the morning, have a long and leisurely lunch at the pub where all the bankers and lawyers met each afternoon, work out at the men's club from four to six, and arrive for dinner on the dot of seven. Wonderful, dependable Joey. Why had I never thought of him as anything but a pal? For that matter, Joey had never taken any romantic interest in me, either. After the death of his wife a few years ago, he had been content to nurture a few close friends without strings. I counted myself fortunate to be one of them. As for anything more. . .well, some things are just never in the program.

I had toyed with the notion of sharing with Joey the experiences of the last three days, but something held me back. Perhaps I just didn't want to get him involved. He'd worry. He might try to interfere. It was my problem, and I was the one who had to decide how to solve it. Besides, the time we'd spent sipping coffee together had been mostly taken up with instructions on how to handle his precious antique car. The more he talked, the more reluctant I became about driving the thing. It was obviously of great value, at least to Joey, and I kept asking if he wouldn't rather just not lend it to me. I was perfectly able to rent a vehicle for a week, I assured him.

But he remained stubborn about my using the classic beast, yet spent a good portion of our half hour together going over, in specific detail, all the do's and don'ts and peculiarities associated with its operation. By the time he'd disappeared on the other side of the old-age complex, I'd resolved to drive the blasted machine as little as possible. Except I had to get the monstrosity off the curb. Grayson, as wide a boulevard as it was, became a narrow lane to the drivers who had to negotiate around the "Silver Dinosaur," a name I'd decided fit the car to a tee.

I brought Joey's keys out of my pocket and walked to the street. Close up, the car sprawled like a shopping mall. I found myself looking up and down Grayson before I opened the door. I was aware of a sudden crawly feeling which I remembered from adolescent days when I'd been demoralized with embarrassment at being picked up outside of junior high school by my mother. What was it about this car? It was a perfectly respectable car . . . "If you like boats," a sneering teen voice replied from somewhere inside my head.

I put the key in the ignition and turned it. Like a charm, the engine sprang to life. Reflexively, I glanced in the rearview mirror as I put my foot on the brake and switched into reverse. The car didn't end where it should have. It stretched on past the back seat, the trunk, and four yards of chrome to where the outboard motor should have been.

I cursed the fact that I had never had any training in driving a tractor-trailer rig. How was I going to steer this football field into the driveway, which only moments ago had been of respectable size but now seemed to have suddenly been short-sheeted?

I had to get over on the other side of the street and make a wide swing. As I began backing up toward the court, I made a mental note to buy one of those bumper stickers for Joey that read "This Car Makes Wide Turns." The car arrived quicker than I'd anticipated, and I began turning the wheel frantically, realizing too late that this was pre-power-steering vintage. I wasn't going to get the car at a neat ninety-degree angle turn into the court. If I didn't stop now, I'd be under Martha's clothesline with the birds and the bread crumbs.

I hit the brake. The car went from a slow rolling glide into instant rigor mortis. For a moment, my body was jammed against the seat with such force that I wondered if there would be a permanent imprint. At the same time, from somewhere behind me, I thought I heard the shriek of a train. Then I realized with embarrassment that it had been the squeal of the tires coming to an instant stop.

Still gripping the wheel, I gave another quick adolescent

look around me and assessed my position. The car was sprawled at a slant across the court about forty degrees off of my intended ninety. Luckily, no one seemed to be around. Why was I thankful that that included Nick Michaels? Who cared what Peeping Toms thought of my driving prowess? Then I remembered it was his car I had wrecked, and a judge might be interested in this little misadventure with Joey's whale.

Regardless, I took a deep breath and put the car into first gear, then inched out onto Grayson, attaining the right-hand side just before coming opposite my driveway. I began turning the sluggish steering wheel with all the muscles I could call upon while my foot did the two-step on the sensitive brake pedal. Just when I thought I had the car into the driveway, I looked behind to find the last half acre still sitting on the sidewalk. I limped the car forward again until I was as close to the garage door as I could get without making it a permanent hood ornament.

With great relief, I put the thing in park and shut off the engine. I was even more relieved to find, upon standing on firm ground once again, that the car had managed to clear the sidewalk acceptably, and the driver's seat had not retained an impression of my backside.

For the rest of the morning, I vowed never to drive the car again as I worked to keep myself cool in the debilitating heat wave. As soon as my insurance office opened, I called with news of the accident and Nick's information. But mostly, I tried to resume my thinking about the events of the last three days. I came up with one constant: nothing unusual had happened before Franny's arrival. Whatever was going had been introduced by Franny's moving in. If I knew why Franny was the trigger, everything else would fall into a sensible place.

There was also no doubt left in my mind that Nick and Franny knew each other, and that Nick was involved, as well. But involved in what?

Was this a love-affair thing? Had Franny given Nick a key to the house? Was this just an innocent attempt to get to the second floor to be with her?

But Franny hadn't been home last night, and why grab me

and hold me hostage even for a short period of time?

Brut, the anguished tone repeated in my head.

I slipped into my bathing suit and went out to the pool to cool off. It was now eleven o'clock and ninety-five degrees. It was becoming difficult to even think straight.

I found myself wondering where Terrance was in this heat. I hadn't thought much about him with all the other confusion taking up my time, but his dog run sat blatantly still and added just one more question to my troubled list of concerns.

I floated and lolled for a while, enjoying the momentary escape from the oppressive temperature. Eventually, I began thinking about frying some chicken and creating the potato salad.

I sat and air-dried at the umbrella table and stared at Nick's house. I wondered where he had been going this morning, and realized that I still didn't know what he did for work. "I hope to go on vacation starting tomorrow," I remembered him saying. In normal jobs you knew when vacations started; they weren't just hoped for.

Did he have a business of his own? Was he a lawyer about to close an important case? Was he a con man hoping to pull off the big job and hide out for a while?

I shivered with that thought and walked through the ninety-eight-degree high-noon heat into the house.

I turned on the tiny portable television on my kitchen counter to watch the midday news while I peeled potatoes.

"We go to Gina Day at Great Lake," anchorman Curtis Goode was saying.

I thought of Jana having a wonderful day over at Great Lake Park as the peeler made a husky whisper against the potatoes.

"Curtis," Gina's own husky voice droned, "firemen from three neighboring communities will continue dragging the lake today looking for Percy Hapinsky's body."

I froze and turned to regard the blonde reporter's face on the tiny screen. Happy's name! Could this be his grandson, who shared the name Percy with his grandfather?

"Some young people were reportedly swimming illegally in the warm, early hours of dawn," Gina continued. "When they gathered everyone for the trip home, Percy Hapinsky was missing. It is feared that he has drowned."

The station went back to Curtis Goode and a new headline. Mechanically, I resumed peeling potatoes, but I couldn't get the story out of my head. They hadn't mentioned where the victim was from. Perhaps with all the confusion there, they had not ascertained any more details.

I had just set the pan of potatoes on the stove and snapped on the burner when a brief squeal from up the street erupted and died, and my television went dead, as well. I walked through the foyer to the front door. Everything suddenly seemed so quiet, and I realized the drone of the air conditioners from the old-age home had stopped.

"Obviously a power outage," I mused and hoped it wouldn't last long.

But it did.

At one-thirty, I removed the uncooked potatoes from the top of the stove, drained them, and stored them in a container on a shelf in my refrigerator.

The heat was worse. My thermometer on the deck said a hundred and three degrees. Even if the electricity came on now, it would be terribly uncomfortable to cook. I had no choice but to run to the deli and pick up the potato salad and fried chicken. I knew what dessert would be: all we could eat of the two half gallons of ice cream that would be melting in the freezer if the power was not on by dinnertime.

There was only one problem. The deli was three blocks away, and in this heat I'd be a fool to walk it. I'd have to drive the Silver Dinosaur.

I cheered up by reminding myself that the three blocks were in a straight line from here. The only turning would be in the parking lot. If I made wide turns, how difficult could it be?

Without depressing myself by answering my own stupid question, I threw on a shirt and a pair of shorts, grabbed my pocketbook, locked the house, and climbed into the infernal machine. I waited until no cars were in sight and backed out onto Grayson. Of course, the car was pre-air-conditioning vintage, too, and by the time I had wrestled with the steering to maneuver it into heading straight down the three blocks, and had worked at cranking down the driver's side pre-electric window, I was a mass of sweat. I felt as if I had run the three blocks, and I hadn't even driven them yet.

At each intersection, I had to stop to check for traffic and was proud that I had remembered to tap the brake ever so gently and well ahead of time. At the first stop, I looked to my right toward Happy's house but did not see any sign of activity. I hoped that meant that the drowning victim had not been his grandson.

I arrived at the deli and selected the furthest space, well away from any other parked cars. I felt slimy with perspiration, and my hair was crimped from the humidity. All I wanted to do was get in and out as quickly as possible. Unfortunately, other people had made the same decision about tonight's menu, so I stood in line and waited my turn. By the time I was back in the car, it was two-thirty.

The brief three-block ride was uneventful until I reached the last intersection before my house. Several cars were lined up around Happy's— too many to be normal.

Preoccupied by this new development, I forgot to tap the brake when I reached my driveway, and I hit it too hard, sending the car into sudden death, my body into the steering wheel this time, and the tires into an ungodly wail that I was sure could be heard in Chelsea, ten miles away.

Totally humiliated, I crawled into the driveway, knocked the four feet of frontal chrome against the garage to be sure I was tucked in sufficiently, and got myself into the house as quickly and as invisibly as I could.

I stored the chicken and salad in a large pot amidst additional chunks of ice I had purchased and thought about Happy. How could I find out if the victim had indeed been his grandson? I arranged space for the pot on the bottom shelf of the refrigerator and went to the phone.

Unbelievably, for the fourth time in four days, my phone connected me to the police. I introduced myself and asked, first, about the extent of the power outage. I was surprised to learn that not only was the city totally involved, but the entire eastern seaboard. "Too many air conditioners," the desk sergeant explained.

Then I told him that I had heard some sad news just before we lost electricity. As a neighbor, I wanted to do something for the family if the victim of that drowning had been Happy's grandson. The officer was very kind, very sympathetic as he confirmed my fears.

I thanked him and was about to hang up when I remembered something. "Sergeant," I said, "while I have you on the phone, has anything new developed since last night regarding the area's Peeping Tom?"

"Peeping Tom?" he echoed, sounding surprised. "I don't recall any Peeping Tom report for anywhere in the city. Just a minute and I'll check the logs."

There was a substantial pause before the sergeant returned to the phone. "No, Ma'am," he said, "there've been no complaints along those lines anywhere in town."

"But last night when my boarder, Franny Gardner, called to complain about a prowler, an officer on the desk revealed there'd been a rash of Peeping-Tom incidents in the Grayson Street area," I insisted.

"What time did she speak to the desk?" he asked.

When I told him it had been about midnight, there was another stretch of silence before he spoke again.

"Are you certain about the time?" he inquired. "Things were fairly quiet after eleven-thirty last night. None of the calls that did come in within that time frame were about prowlers. Three traffic mishaps and a fire over on the north side. Somebody's telling stories," he ended.

I mumbled something about misunderstanding, and in my haste to disconnect, I fairly slammed down the receiver. I was trembling. Franny hadn't called the police last night. But she had talked for at least ten minutes to someone.

Or had she been talking to an empty line for my benefit?

Why?

I remembered how she had not wanted me to call the police.

Why?

Of course, I had no answer to any of the whys. At least not yet.

What I did have, however, was some recourse. Whatever was going on, Franny was certainly involved, which made her staying with me impossible from this very moment on. When Franny reported to the restaurant tonight, I would call her and inform her that she was not to return here after work. I'd arrange to have her things sent wherever she directed, but I would make it clear that I didn't want her back in my home again.

Making that decision somehow freed me to examine, more easily, other options at my disposal. Franny still had a key, of course, and she had possibly given keys to others, as well. I dialed a local locksmith and persuaded him that it was crucial that the locks on my two steel doors be changed before nightfall.

Fortunately, the type and manufacturer of my locks were standard ones, and therefore, Miles Locksmithing was able to complete the installation by five o'clock. I breathed a sigh of relief as I watched the truck pull away and felt the only copies of the brand-new keys secure in my hands.

CHAPTER 11

I took a quick shower, towel-dried my hair, pulled on the coolest and simplest summer dress I owned, applied the barest essentials of makeup, and left to pay my respects to Happy and Sarah.

Cars now lined both sides of Grayson and one small side street. The front door stood open as I approached, and I followed an elderly couple into the modest hallway.

Happy stood at the living room archway greeting his friends and neighbors. I gave him a kiss on the cheek as we silently shook hands. He had the same jaw set he had when he was jogging or biking, and I realized that he must be summoning the same determination to cope with this tragedy that he used to endure his arduous physical routine.

Beyond Happy in the darkened living room, Sarah sat like a stone figure in the middle of a couch. People were on either side of her, but they did not seem to be giving her much attention, at least at the moment, so I moved toward her and leaned over to take both her hands and make eye contact.

"Sarah," I said, "you remember me, don't you? Janet Connors. I live in your son's house now."

I thought I saw a flicker of recognition before tears began rolling down the old lady's cheeks.

"My poor children," Sarah wept, shaking her head from side to side.

I dropped to my knees, still holding one of Sarah's hands. A woman sitting to her left tucked a tissue into her right one, but she didn't seem to notice. She just kept shaking her head while the tears slid off her cheeks onto her arms.

I searched for something of comfort to say to the woman.

"Your son and daughter-in-law will be coming home today, I hope," I said to her.

"He's dead," she sobbed. "Now they're all dead."

Alarmed at her despair and confusion, I took the tissue from her hand and began patting her cheeks. The woman to her right put an arm around her shoulders, and I smiled faintly in the woman's direction.

Sarah pulled a little away from her embrace and leaned toward me. "Be careful," she whispered. Her crying seemed to have stopped for now. I patted her hand and would have released it and gotten to my feet, but she grasped my hand so tightly that I was sure her fingers were leaving a mark on my skin. "He's killed them all now," she nodded with a sudden taciturn expression that sent a chill up my back.

I was managing to release myself from her grip when a pair of strong hands under my elbows lifted me to my feet. I turned to regard Happy whose gaze was fixed on his wife's face. "Sarah needs to rest," he said simply, and, reaching in front of me, he pulled his wife to her feet and began leading her out of the room.

"Be careful," she said over her shoulder to me as she was led away.

"It's a shame," one woman on the couch commented.

"She has no idea," another said, shaking her head and clicking her tongue.

With my small duty done, I escaped from the morbid scene and breathed a sigh of relief when I was outside in the light once more.

When I thought about Sarah, it was with a rush of great despair because she suffered far more in the depths of her confused mind than Happy did in the face of his singular tragic reality. I wondered what was being done for Sarah's poor, tormented soul. Certainly medication, but was that enough?

I resolved to visit Sarah more often and perhaps bring her to my home from time to time, where she had seemed to find some peace in the past.

It was only five-thirty when I used my new key for the first time and let myself into the house. The phone was ringing.

"Mom," came my daughter's excited voice when I answered. "I'm at McDonald's in Cambridge with Laurie. Is it possible to pick us up here in an hour? Sharon's having a birthday party, and she's invited us to stay for cake and ice cream, but Mr. Burgess has to get the van back and unloaded. If you can't do it, it's okay, Mom, but I wanted to ask."

McDonald's would be a tricky ride across town and into Cambridge with an army tank. "I can do it," I said. My heart had melted at my daughter's mature appeal, and after all, the Burgesses had just completed a twenty- four-hour odyssey for their children and Jana. The least I could do was pick them up from a birthday party, Silver Dinosaur or not!

"Oh, Mom," Jana's voice kept the excited pace, "guess who we saw at the park this morning? Franny!"

"Franny?" I echoed.

"Guess who she was with?"

I was still too busy grappling with the idea of Franny being at the park to respond. I had expected Jana to report the drowning, but obviously, she hadn't yet heard about it. *Just as well*, I thought.

"The Disco King!" was the breathless response. "Franny knows the Disco King! Guess who wants an introduction!"

"Uh, Laurie," I answered smugly.

"Well, yeah, her too," Jana laughed. "Gotta run, Mom. Love you."

There was a click before I could reply. I hung up the phone feeling a warm flush. It was a sensation that a week ago I would have said I'd never feel after a conversation with my daughter. She was suddenly different, I realized. The accident had frightened her. She'd been away overnight, too. Had she been homesick? A little?

I calculated the time. I had to pick Jana up at six-thirty. Joey would be here on the dot of seven. That would be a stretch. I called him and left a message on his machine to make it seven-thirty instead and told him why.

At a quarter of six, I took another quick shower and changed to a more sporty short pants outfit for the evening and dinner on the deck. I had time to get some lanterns and candles together on the dining room table in case the electricity hadn't returned by dark. The back upper and lower decks would be well lighted by the array of citronella candles already placed strategically on them and around the pool.

A little after six, I dialed Franny at work. She'd be there by now, and I was anxious to have this unpleasant task over with. Since Jana's call, I hadn't been able to get Franny off my mind. I kept thinking how ironic it was that she was involved with the man across the court whom I had been infatuated with, and now, it would seem, with *Jana's* teenage heartthrob, as well.

"Dick's Grill," a man announced gruffly on the second ring.

I introduced myself and asked if I could have a brief word with Franny Gardner.

"Franny Gardner!" came the hoarse retort punctuated by a sound that was half laugh and half cough. "Ain't that a hoot! Franny ain't been workin' here since a week and a half ago when she just plain never showed up again. You tell her highness that—"

I hung up in the middle of the man's tirade. Why was I surprised?

"I'm going right to work tonight," she had said this morning.

So it's just another lie, though not as serious as the lie about calling the police and the one about the Peeping Tom, I mused.

My decision to change the locks today was even more gratifying at this moment.

I grabbed my keys and my purse and headed for the door. Through the screen I was surprised to see Happy about to ring the bell.

"Happy, hi," I said. "What can I do for you? Is Sarah all right?"

"I was going to ask you to sit with her for a bit while the rest of the family makes some of the arrangements," he said.

"Oh, dear, Happy, I'm just leaving to pick up Jana. I'm sorry."

I stepped onto the front stoop and shut the door behind me.

"It's okay, Kiddo," Happy said as I inserted the key into the bolt lock.

"Here, let me help you," he said, reaching for the key and re-opening the door briefly, then slamming it shut. He braced himself while he turned the tumbler with some force. "All secure, Kiddo," was his parting comment as he removed the key and handed it back.

I watched him move in his energetic way down the walk and toward the old-age home, his mind already focused on his problem of finding someone to sit with Sarah.

CHAPTER 12

I got across town with little effort. I was beginning to get a feel for the car. Sometimes, though, I would have the sense that I was being followed. I kept doing a double-take in my rearview mirror, and when I'd find the road empty behind me I couldn't believe it. I was finding it difficult to comprehend that I was being tailgated by my own tail fins!

About a block from McDonald's, I stopped at a light and began to reflect on the assortment of lies Franny had been feeding me. The deception had started with her failure to mention Terrance. Terrance. He'd been gone for a full day now. If he returned, I'd have a motherless dog on my hands. The thought made me chuckle. It also distracted me completely, and I almost drove right by McDonald's.

Without thinking, I jammed on the brakes. Above the normal roar of traffic sailed a locomotive-like scream of tires as the dinosaur stopped dead, throwing me—once again—into the steering wheel. I looked to my left and saw Jana and all her party friends lined up under the arches waiting for their respective rides, laughing and pointing in my direction. As I turned into the parking lot, the group stared incredulously as the car that had made a spectacle of itself advanced toward them. I knew when Jana recognized me because her eyes widened, her mouth gaped, and she assumed the Dicky Dunlap salute.

"Where did you get *this?*" she gasped as she and Laurie piled into the back seat.

I'm sure she wished she could disappear. The rest of the girls waved a good-bye with one hand and tee-heed behind the other, staring at us all the while we were pulling away.

"Why?" I asked, looking into the rearview mirror at Laurie and my daughter, shrunken in size against the huge cavern of upholstery. "It's a nice car."

"Mo...om!" wailed Jana.

I laughed as I explained the arrangement with Joey in regard to the Silver Dinosaur.

Then I listened, without comment, as Jana reported their Franny sighting.

"We were on the wall by the beach when the Disco King rode by on the boulevard with Franny in the passenger seat. She had a kerchief on, but it was definitely Franny," Jana told me.

I remembered what she'd been wearing this morning—she'd been all dressed up.

"Describe her outfit," I said.

"I don't know, Mom," came the familiar, impatient reply. "It was Franny, wasn't it, Laurie?"

"She had a red top on," Laurie contributed.

I remembered that red top. What in hell would Franny be doing with a teenaged boy? As soon as I had wondered that, I recalled her strange assortment of suitors up to now. On second thought, the unsightly Disco King fit right in.

I pulled the Silver Dinosaur up the driveway as slick as you please, and the girls and I alighted. It had already been decided that Jana was going to sleep over at Laurie's to relive the events of the last twenty-four hours. Her things were still over at the Burgesses' so she and Laurie went directly there, chattering excitedly all the way, as I suspected they would continue to do for most of the night.

When I opened the door, I was glad the children had not come into the house. I stared incredulously at the most god-awful sight I had ever witnessed. Someone had been here in my brief absence and trashed, thrown, and otherwise heaped everything out of drawers and off of shelves. I gazed in disbelief at the piles of debris on the floor of each room on the lower level.

I didn't touch anything. Leaving the front door open, I went to the kitchen and dialed 911. The troops were there in riot fashion in less than five minutes. This time I was glad to see them.

"I had all new locks installed earlier today," I told the now-familiar sergeant. He just shook his head.

"You have to use them," he said sarcastically.

"The back slider was open when I came home," I said. "Could that have been the point of entry?"

"Not if you really had the bar down." He showed me the cross-piece still straight and intact.

"I know it was down," I said weakly. "And I know the other doors were locked, too."

We were in the dining room. All of my dishes, usually in the hutch and buffet, had been thrown out into the middle of the room. Most were broken.

"What about there?" I pointed to the open and screened window on the side wall over my buffet.

"The screen isn't forced," the sergeant said with a tone that I thought reflected impatience.

"Who else has a key?" he asked.

"These locks aren't three hours old," I told him. "I've given no one a key."

"Who put 'em in?"

I gave him the name of the company.

The sergeant nodded. "Good reliable firm," he said and didn't even write down the name.

Upstairs was worse because every bit of bedding, clothing, and linen had been thrown from beds and closets.

"Someone was looking for something," the sergeant said. "Do you have any idea what anyone would be looking for in your home?" His eyes had narrowed and his voice had taken on a suspicious edge.

"I wish I did," I sighed, looking away.

The sergeant radioed for a photographer. I was surprised that out of the crowd of policemen who always showed up there wasn't already every specialist from photographer to forensics.

I had, of course, forgotten about the time, and suddenly Joey was standing in the middle of Jana's room with the rest of us. All her cabinets of stuffed animals and records had been dumped. Her bookcases, though not toppled, had had their contents thrown around the room. Her Elvis memorabilia was also trashed. I didn't dare inspect closely to see if the important figurines were harmed. There would be time for that later, when I felt stronger. Right now I felt raped as I regarded all my family's personal and private contents, if not smashed, at least violated.

"What you need to do," the sergeant was saying, "is make a list of all items damaged or missing and report this to your insurance company."

I nodded numbly, thinking of the hours it would take to clean the place up, never mind pausing to make lists as I went along. It was dusk when the officers climbed into their respective cruisers and left the street single file. Joey and I watched them in silence from Jana's front bedroom window.

Outside, behind us in the court, in Laurie's driveway, I could hear Jana and Laurie and a group of their friends skipping rope to the popular jingle of the summer:

> I don't want to party,
> And I don't want to sing,
> I want to go dancing
> With the Disco King.

For a moment I pictured the long, swinging cord and the girls lined up to take their turns at jumping in to recite their own verses.

> When I get to be a woman
> With a dowry to bring,
> I want to get married
> To the Disco King.

I was relieved that none of them had seen the cruisers on Grayson. I could draw comfort in knowing that Jana had been busy spinning tales of her park adventures and the sighting of her Disco King hero instead of being dragged into this utter devastation. I envied all of them as I listened to their voices full of joy.

When I get old
And I've done everything,
I want to go to heaven
With the Disco King.

Joey hadn't said a word since I'd first seen him standing in the middle of the room with a dumbfounded look on his face. Now he turned, and if I hadn't been so upset, I would have cracked up laughing at his first statements.

"I didn't know this city had so many cops," he said, and followed that with another equally perceptive gem: "I wouldn't think they would send all their men out on one call. I would think it would be like fire trucks—you leave a few in the station in case of another emergency."

I had a feeling that if I allowed myself to laugh right then, I'd never stop. And I didn't have time to be hysterical. Yet.

"What are you going to do first?" he asked, looking around the room.

A tiny suggestion of a breeze had begun drifting through Jana's southerly window, reminding me of how hot I was.

"First, we swim," I said. "Then we eat. I can't clean up most of this mess in the dark, which will be upon us in a few minutes. I'll have to wait until daylight for that."

I was thankful that the potato salad container had remained intact from a spill out of the refrigerator, and most of the fried chicken had not escaped its wrapping when it was hurled to the kitchen floor.

Joey changed into his trunks in the downstairs bathroom, which, with the exception of the toilet cover, had not been disturbed.

"What did they think they would find in the toilet tank?" Joey chuckled as he came out moments later.

"*Gold*fish," I replied dryly, emphasizing the *gold*.

Joey rewarded me with his infectious laugh. "I picked up the pieces," he said. "They're in the wastebasket in there. Whoever did this just threw off the top and let it smash to the floor."

While I changed into my bathing suit upstairs, Joey lit the

citronella candles on the decks and the ones I'd left on the dining room table. They had somehow remained untouched.

"Whoever it was, was definitely looking for something," Joey mused as we tiptoed around the debris on the first floor, placing the lights in strategic locations. "If they had just been trashing for kicks, they would have knocked these candles over, too." While the world grew dark and the flickering of the flames grew brighter against it, Joey and I swam and sipped on gin-and-tonics. Over a cold dinner that tasted remarkably good, I finally filled Joey in on everything that had happened since Franny had arrived. He was a good audience. He laughed in the right places and bemoaned my dilemmas when appropriate.

Through the whole replay of events, I watched the shimmer of eerie lights from the decks reflect in the blackened windows of my house, giving the scene a Halloweenish effect.

"You can't stay here tonight," Joey said when I had finished my story. "Come to my place. I'll take the sofa."

"Thanks, but no," I told him. "I can't run away. This is my home."

"But until the police find out what is going on. . ."

I was shaking my head no. "I have to stay," I said in a tone that Joey correctly interpreted as final.

We ate bowls of ice cream and swam a few more times. During the evening, a spectacular full moon crept over the pool and added an additional glow to the night. If I had not known what chaos lay inside my house, had it not been for the macabre lighting throwing flares and shadows against the windows of the rooms, had I not been consumed with unanswered and troublesome questions, it would have been a totally soft and gentle evening.

Around eleven, Joey insisted on escorting me through the house with a flashlight as I checked each entrance. He left by the front door and waited on the stoop as I double-bolted the new locks. I stood in the darkened foyer as he tried the door from his side.

"Okay," I heard him say. "Call me at any sign of trouble," was his last directive. I heard him start up his car and saw his headlights through the front window as they led him out of Grayson Street.

CHAPTER 13

I turned and confronted my home.
 Candles flickered in the darker corners, and light from the moon splashed through the archway between the living room and dining room. The foyer and stairway where I was and the kitchen beyond were in total darkness. I raised my eyes to where I knew the stairs were and missed the spidery webs of light that usually emanated from the burglar alarm and sprinkled the hallway with colorful patterns.

The reality of my aloneness hit me, and for the first time I felt myself give way to fear. I inched toward the lighted archway and took up a position at the dining room table by the slider. Perhaps it was because this spot had not been touched by whoever had ransacked the house, that I opted to take up a vigil there. I did not entertain for a moment going to bed upstairs. I wouldn't be able to sleep with such a mess around me. No, I'd sit here as long as I could stay awake and then, perhaps, lie down on the living room couch. Two narrow windows in the living room on either side of the bay would admit a bit of a breeze.

From where I sat, I could see, in the moonlight, that the battery-operated clock registered a little after midnight. *Five hours to dawn*, I thought.

My mind began to wander. Had I remembered to shut off the burner under the potatoes when I put them away this afternoon? I grabbed my flashlight and went out to the kitchen. The burner was off. I went back and sat down.

I wondered if I should blow out the candles in this room and the next. I decided I'd feel better in the dark, so I took another few minutes to walk around extinguishing the flames. My one large flashlight guided me back to my seat at the table.

No sooner had I sat back down than I heard a slight sound outside behind me. I turned and, through the slider, saw Nick Michaels and the blonde woman who had been rude to me the day before come out of his house into the moonlight.

They walked briskly down the steps, and I was surprised when they did not turn toward his driveway, but continued walking up the court toward Grayson.

I moved silently to the open screened window and crouched. I could hear his voice and then hers, but I couldn't pick up any words. When they got to the end of my fence, I could see that they hadn't changed their brisk pace. I hoped I was crouched low enough and out of the moonlight so as to be totally hidden while I kept watching and listening.

Their tone was rather dull, and I sensed they were keeping their voices purposely low. It was impossible to catch even an occasional word until they were at the sidewalk by my window. It was Nick who spoke my name. I clearly heard "Janet" and then the name Franny.

Had I only heard *my* name, I could have persuaded myself that there were hundreds of Janets he could have been referring to. But coupled with the name Franny, I knew he was talking about me. As he spoke the names, the woman turned to look in my direction. Her head was angled upward toward the bedroom window above the spot where I crouched. Franny's room! (Franny's *former* room!)

As I gazed directly on her face, I was struck once again by a feeling of familiarity. Where had I seen her before? As quickly as they were walking, they were already beyond me at the corner.

Carefully, I eased my way to the front bay window. I was in darkness more now because of the absence of moonlight, and I risked crawling onto the couch and getting closer to the small screened side window. If they turned right, I would not see them. But if they turned left, they would be in my view as soon as they got past my hedges and azaleas.

I heard their voices before I saw them. As they appeared in

front of me again, the woman turned once more toward me in a sweeping regard of my house, and I suddenly remembered! I'd seen her before, all right! Inside the antique vehicle that had been exiting the garage at the boarded-up houses! It was the woman with the long harsh face who'd been driving the old Studebaker.

In an instant, I was off the couch. They were hurrying past my house after midnight. My bet was that they were headed for those houses!

I remembered Franny being sure that Terrance was trapped inside one of them. Was he there again now? Who were those strange people, and what was my handsome neighbor's affiliation with them?

Groping in the dark for the shelf where I kept the keys, I grabbed both sets and opened the front door. Through the screen, I could see them just about to turn the corner by Peddington's. I snapped the inside lock and closed the door. It took some fumbling to find the key that would fit the bolt lock, and I lost several precious seconds. Never mind; I'd take the shortcut to Sawyer Boulevard.

By now, the two figures were out of sight. I raced across the street, lighted by the moon, and did not slow my pace until I reached the other side of the old-age complex by crossing, as Joey had done earlier, under the archways.

I turned left as I came out on Sawyer. The street was empty. I had to assume that Nick and his girlfriend were now at, or even in, the boarded-up houses.

I am not a courageous person, and I did not intend to get caught. My main objective was to overhear enough to put some pieces together that would answer at least a few of my questions. It appeared that my home had become part of something sinister. With Franny no longer having access to it, maybe I could live in peace again. But I had to be sure. I had to arm myself with more information in order to have some peace of mind. Maybe the police could be of more help to me if I found out, for example, what the intruder had been searching for.

As I moved up the street, another voice of concern tugged at the back of my mind. I'd been in a hurry this afternoon. Happy had been in a hurry. Perhaps he had accidentally failed to secure the door. For a moment, I paused on the dark stone sidewalk and tried to remember if he had tested the door as I had just done to be sure the bolt was in place. I couldn't remember. But what difference did that make? Someone had, by whatever means, gotten into my house. I needed not to know *how* they got in as much as *why* they would want to. I started to walk again. Slowly.

I stayed on the left sidewalk of Sawyer Boulevard until I was opposite the two boarded-up Colonials on the other side of the street. This way, I would not risk being seen from the only unboarded window on the side of the second floor of the first house.

No streetlights guided me tonight. There was no light except for the moon, which had begun dipping in and out of fair-weather clouds. It would help me find my way behind the matted hedge, and, by the same token, could expose me as the trespasser I surely was. I needed to be patient, quiet, and careful!

As I made my way across the street, I tried to remember where the hedge stopped on the left side of the houses. I headed up the sidewalk toward an area that, in the moonlight, seemed less dark and therefore, I guessed, less dense.

Then I waited for another cloud.

All was unnaturally still. No cars passed me while I lingered by the hedge. Without electricity, there was no background music or chatter from a late- night radio or television emanating from the open windows of the homes that lined this populated boulevard. That's why, when I heard the sound of a heavy door closing quietly, I could fix it precisely beyond where I stood. Someone had just entered or exited the boarded-up house on the left—the one I stood directly in front of with only the hedge between. I strained to hear the sound of footsteps or voices or the snap of a twig, but the utter silence returned.

A cloud dimmed the moon, but I froze where I was. What if someone was standing, as I was, listening on the front step of the house? If I ventured around the hedge, I'd be heard by anyone waiting in the yard, and even in a darkened state of the moon, I'd be a moving shape to eyes that had grown somewhat accustomed to the absence of light.

The moon reappeared, and I continued to wait. I thought about just moving back across Sawyer Boulevard and going home. So what if I were heard or seen on a public street? It was when I crossed into a private yard that I'd be trespassing. So far I hadn't broken any laws. I could just go home. But my home was trashed, and I was now even afraid to be there. I had to get answers. That was my only defense.

The moon ducked behind another cloud, and I ducked through the hedge.

I was standing openly in front of one of the boarded houses!

If anyone were in the yard, they would have heard me breaking through the dry brush under the hedge. I froze again to listen for any sound of corresponding movement. There was none. So eventually, I moved up against the front side of the house.

The moon lost its cover, and the yard and I could no longer hide. The light afforded me a view of both front yards.

They were empty.

Keeping myself flat against the house, I moved toward the side of it and peered cautiously around its corner. All was clear, and I continued toward the rear. Again, when I reached the backyard, I looked carefully around the corner before I stepped out. Like the front yards, the back area was also empty, but I thought a thin patch of light glowed at the edge of the house furthest away. I looked to see if streetlights were back on, thinking that the outage could have been finally corrected, but except for the moon, all was dark. Keeping myself against the house, I worked my way across the backyard.

I was listening for voices the whole time and beginning to wonder if this whole excursion was for nothing. Then, as I reached the end of the first house, the moon clouded over again, and this time there was no doubt that some kind of light was beyond where I stood. It seemed to be coming from the garage on the side of the second house. Cautiously, I kept moving toward the thin illumination.

It was then that I heard voices. By the time I had taken a few more steps, I decided that people were either just outside the garage or inside the opened garage doors. On this hot evening, I imagined this was the only way to get fresh air, with the houses boarded up as they were. I also reasoned that the source of light must be flashlights or candles. I plastered myself against the side of the back wall only inches from the corner and listened.

". . .over now that he's dead," a male voice was saying.

"Not if she's involved," came a second male voice.

"She isn't." This voice had an edge of anger to it. It was also familiar. It was the same tone he had used when he'd said, "Brut." There was no question that I was listening to Nick Michaels.

"You don't know that for a fact," a woman's voice said.

"I know it in my gut," Nick answered, and there was a scraping sound as feet moved across concrete. Then the crunch of gravel as those feet found the driveway.

I tried to press myself closer to the side of the house.

"Where are you going?" I heard the woman ask.

I turned my head in the direction of the footsteps in an effort to hear better. Nick Michaels was standing a little way out and over from the garage. His back was toward me. (For the moment!)

Every inch of my body stiffened as I realized that discovery was only seconds away—as soon as Nick turned around or I bolted and broke my silence by moving.

"I'm restless," he said in answer to the woman's question, and then he turned just as the moon came out from behind another cloud.

"There's nothing we can do now, until the autopsy," the woman said.

Nick had stopped dead in his tracks. He was frozen, as was I, as we stared at each other.

"If they retrieve the body at all," a man's voice replied.

"If there is a body," someone else suggested.

"We were so close to nailing all of them," one of the males in the garage muttered.

Nick Michaels tore his gaze from mine and deliberately turned the other way. "I'm going for a walk," he said.

I listened to his shoes on the gravel drive as his steps receded into the distance.

Was he signaling to the others now that he was out of my

sight? Why hadn't he reacted when he saw me obviously eavesdropping? Two running steps and he'd have been able to drag me from my hiding place.

Sheer panic gripped me and twisted my reasoning. He was, at this moment, circling around and coming in on my other side to surround me, I decided, as if it would take a complex strategy to capture me.

I started to run then, back along the rear yards of the two houses, and I kept going into the backyard of the neighboring house. I didn't look behind me until I turned left and reached the sidewalk of Sawyer Boulevard. In a crouching position, I paused to see if I was being followed. That was when it dawned on me, as I crouched like a fool, that I used to be a sane, responsible mother and teacher.

Sawyer Boulevard was empty. Those in the garage must not have heard me run back along the houses. The grass had been high and soft. With no little relief, I realized it must have cushioned any sound of my departure.

But where was Nick Michaels? He'd gone down the drive but was nowhere to be seen now. Was he doubling back around the houses even now, trying to trap me? Waiting behind the hedges?

Why didn't he grab me when he had the chance? I wondered.

I was in a state of indecision, just standing on the sidewalk at what must be close to one in the morning.

Then a sensible voice somewhere deep inside said, "Start walking."

Which I did. I walked directly across the boulevard and turned squarely left when I got to the opposite sidewalk, keeping my hysteria in check and my pace at a normal rhythm.

I glanced once at the boarded-up houses across the street, and then I was past them.

Just as I reached the old-age home and turned right toward Grayson, he was at my side!

Afterward, I would try to figure out just how he had materialized. Had he been waiting just beyond the intersection across from the houses? I only know he was suddenly walking in step with me. "I'll see you home," he said quietly.

It took every bit of my will to keep from breaking into a run and screaming.

"I know my way home," I snapped back instead.

Michaels didn't respond.

We were nearing the corner of Grayson now, coming up opposite Happy's house. The moon was hidden once again behind some cloud cover, when a movement across the street on the sidewalk caught my attention. Nick Michaels stopped and grabbed my hand. Instinctively, I tried to snatch it away, but it was too late. Nick used his secure grip to throw me off balance and pull me against him.

My hand, still in his, went with his arm around my back, and I was suddenly locked against his chest, my other hand trying without success to push back from his rough embrace.

The moon came out just a bit, and I pulled my head back to lash out verbally at Michaels's assault, but his attention was not on me; it was directed to the opposite sidewalk. With difficulty, because of my twisted position, I moved my head around enough to observe a figure moving briskly down Grayson. It was Happy.

I struggled hard against Nick then, and opened my mouth to call out to my neighbor at the same time. I had a sense that Happy became aware of us, because it seems to me he had started to turn his head in our direction. But if that was so, what he saw in the cloudy moonlight was a couple locked in a close embrace because in a flash, my struggle had been neutralized with one swift crushing hug that pinned me helplessly into Nick's body and stilled my voice with an equally crushing assault of his mouth on mine.

It was not a kiss.

It was an attack.

At first.

Every few seconds, Michaels pulled his head back enough to whisper, first my name, then a command: "Janet, don't fight me." Then his mouth would return to mine. I was sure he sensed, and correctly so, that I would scream if given the chance.

I was no match for Nick Michaels. The initial vise-like grip had obliterated any hope for release, and I soon tired of struggling. And so we were frozen in this grotesque replica of passion until, for a fourth time, he pulled back to speak to me. "Janet, I'm not your enemy," he whispered, still pinning me against him, but looking straight into my eyes. "We're going to stay just like this until Happy is out of sight."

"Why?" I snapped out at him, struggling halfheartedly in what I knew was a futile effort for release.

As I parted my lips to utter the one word question again, Nick must have anticipated a potential scream because his mouth covered mine once more, only this time, with my lips parted slightly, our mouths met in a confrontation that was soft and sexual.

I felt a response go through his body at the same time the delicious fire began to tear through my own. I had forgotten how compelling total passion could be. Without my permission, my body lost its tension as Nick's embrace took on a different strength. Gone was his tension also. His hold was stronger, if that were possible, but there was a malleability about it as his arms embraced instead of imprisoned.

Our mouths lightly caressed, then deeply pressed to the edge of pain, then caressed once more, until we both turned our faces away to breathe.

My head was against his shoulder. I could feel his cheek against the top of my head, his lips kissing my hair. One very large tear rolled across my cheek, and I am sure, in my frustration between anger and sexual need, there would have been more tears, but at that moment, the streetlights flickered and then flared to full glare. At the same time, a shrill burst of music erupted from Happy's house. Nick stiffened. Then we both turned to watch Happy running at breakneck speed back toward his home as the second refrain of "Boogie-Oogie-Oogie" filled the night.

The moment was bizarre. After one in the morning, with screaming rock music, a full moon, and the lingering sensation of being in the arms of a stranger to whom I would suddenly have been willing to give the benefit of all the doubts I'd ever had about him.

"I have to go," he whispered as he released me. He stood for a moment longer and gazed into my eyes. "Get into your house and lock the doors. Don't let anyone in except Franny."

"Franny?" I managed to gasp before Nick about-faced and sprinted diagonally across the two streets and disappeared into the shadows over on Sawyer Boulevard.

The street was suddenly empty except for me. The music had ceased abruptly, and the night was full of silence once more.

My house stood semi-lighted in the opposite direction from where Nick had disappeared. And suddenly, as I stood staring at my home, a feeling of complete vulnerability overtook me, and the panic that had never been far away won out. I broke into a run, clutching the keys in my pocket, fumbling for the bolt key even as I raced toward my house.

I pulled the key from my pocket and took the front steps two at a time.

Shaking uncontrollably now, I tried to connect the key with the bolt lock. Finally, using both hands, I rammed it in and heard the bolt slide loose. Then the agonizing wait as I found the regular key and fit it into the knob. When the knob turned, I stumbled into the foyer, threw my weight against the door, and secured it behind me.

CHAPTER 14

The light under the hood over the stove was casting a cozy glow in the kitchen. The kaleidoscope lights from the burglar alarm upstairs were once again dancing along the stairway to my right. From outside, I had seen other rooms lighted upstairs, and while I was curious as to what lights I would have left on before the electricity had gone off, I could not bring myself to go upstairs right now.

I stormed through the three rooms downstairs, activating every light on that level. I don't know why I felt compelled to do that. It only served to illuminate the ghastly piles of debris that needed order.

That made me decide to go to work immediately. If I kept busy I would not be able to think about who had trashed my house, coming in somehow through locked doors.

But mostly, I would not think about Nick Michaels' kiss; his arms; his breath against my hair; the very delicious smell of his nearness. I dared not think about him until I had better control of my emotions.

I started with the kitchen. First, I returned pots and pans to their lower cabinets after I had made sure that no shattered glass had affected them or their space. Then I unceremoniously brushed and swept the glass off counters and into garbage cans. I picked up the bigger shards from the floor and then vacuumed the rest. There was glass everywhere. My porcelain stove had been chipped when cups and dishes from above were thrown out of cupboards. I saved nothing in the kitchen in terms of glassware, and kept the required list of losses.

By the time I'd finished the kitchen, it was two-thirty A.M. I hauled my garbage cans and vacuum to the dining room and began working on cleaning up what was left of my china and table linens. The linens were fine, but most of my Lenox collection would need replacing. For some reason, a cup survived and a soup bowl, but the bulk of the service for eight was either chipped or shattered completely.

As I sat at the table refolding linens, my mind rambled again. I remembered Nick's face when he'd caught me eavesdropping at the boarded-up houses. Then I tried to remember the conversation I'd heard there, and I couldn't recall it. What I could recall was the force of Nick's kisses and then the tenderness, and his eyes burning into my own as he instructed me to lock myself into my house. The emptiness of the night, of my spirit, when he suddenly was gone.

I left the linens scattered on the table and moved my cleaning paraphernalia into the living room. There I threw myself into the heavy tasks of picking up the remnants of my belongings in that room—righting furniture, replacing books on shelves, accounting for knickknacks and even sheet music from the overturned piano bench, and focusing on anything but the remnants of passion which the thought of Nick Michaels kindled.

While I was engaged in closely inspecting the figurines and pictures that had been tossed from the walls and piano, I heard a sound above me. I looked up and followed the creak of floorboards with my eyes on the ceiling, starting at the fireplace and then unmistakably moving outward toward the center of the room over my head. *Franny's room*, I remember thinking as I stood holding a figurine with a frozen grip.

The sound of the front screen door opening, and then the scrape of metal on metal at the steel door brought me to full alert.

My first thought, of course, was the intruder. Stealthily, I crept toward the brightly lighted front hall and regarded the knob and the door as someone tried to jiggle both. It was the continued sound of scraping metal, followed by the doorbell, that brought me out of my panic, and with a rush of relief, I demanded, "Who is it?"

I knew, of course, it must be Franny.

"What happened to the locks?" came her familiar voice through the door.

"They've been changed," I said cryptically.

Don't let anyone in except Franny, I heard Nick say.

"I was broken into today, Franny. Whoever did it made a mess of the place. I don't want anyone here until I know what's going on. That includes you. Your boyfriend's over at the boarded-up houses. I'm sure he'll take you in."

There was total silence on the other side of the door, and I imagined Franny processing all that I had just reeled off.

Then I heard the screen door slam and a car at the curb start up. I should have felt relief, but the feeling of my aloneness returned with more intensity.

I stood for at least a minute in the glare of my chandelier as if I were carved in stone in the center of my foyer. Then, with conscious effort, I shook off my stupor and returned to the living room. The figurine I had been studying when Franny arrived was still in my hand, and I returned it to the top of the piano and gazed up at the ceiling.

Had the sound of Franny's arrival somehow been transferred there? Had it triggered the creaking sound a few minutes ago? When only silence answered my questions, I shrugged and went back to the tasks at hand.

Ten minutes later, I had the living room vacuumed and was ready to move on. I hesitated and looked toward the stairs. I listened hard and heard nothing, but something inside of me did not want to ascend those stairs.

"Ridiculous," I said out loud, but I still didn't move. I stood there remembering the shadow in the upstairs hall only a little over twenty-four hours before. Then I thought about the mess and clutter which waited for me on the second level. I scolded myself for being fearful in my own house. That finally did the trick, because what was I doing letting myself feel trapped on the bottom floor of my own home? As silently as possible, I climbed the stairway.

A light burned down the hall in Franny's room. Had she forgotten to extinguish it when she left early this morning? All the other rooms were in darkness.

Beginning with my room, I began turning every light on as I cautiously stepped over the piles of bedding and clothing strewn about. I proceeded down the hall, flipping switches and lighting every corner of each room. I hesitated in front of Franny's partially opened door. One of the police officers must have left it ajar, I assumed. Through the opening, I could see that a lamp on Franny's bedside table was the source of the room's illumination. I pushed the door all the way open and stepped inside.

Debris lay in clumps beside empty cartons, just as I remembered from the previous evening when the police had investigated. Franny must have been mostly packed when she had left on what would now be yesterday morning.

Yesterday morning! It seemed days ago!

I walked slowly around Franny's stripped bed, flicking on lights as I went, until I reached the desk lamp still upright in front of the twin windows overlooking Grayson Street. As I leaned over to snap on the switch, I saw a familiar figure moving quickly along the sidewalk.

I estimated that it must now be near four in the morning. Where was Happy going at this time of night? For that matter, where had he been going at one o'clock when the lights came on? Was he having trouble sleeping tonight because of the tragedy? Because of Sarah?

The closet door stood mostly open at my left, and as I snapped on the desk lamp, a vague sound came from that direction. Every hair on my body bristled, and my heart started pumping wildly.

I stood within a foot of Franny's closet, peering into it, expecting to see an intruder crouched there, ready to spring.

Except for more debris and a couple of boxes, nothing seemed unusual. I moved a step closer and opened the sliding door fully. I was reaching for the string of the closet light when I realized there already was a dim light illuminating the debris on the floor. With reluctance, I forced myself to look up, and my breath caught in my throat.

The ceiling panel that blocked the attic entrance had been

moved aside, and through that exposure glowed the attic light. In horror, I stood transfixed as a shadow moved across that light!

I fled then, around the bed and out the bedroom door. A thumping sound behind me signaled the movement of the person in the attic. In my fright, I raced, not toward the stairs to seek an exit, but toward the darkness of the only unlighted upstairs room, my den—"my sanctuary," as I often affectionately referred to it.

Too late I remembered from this afternoon's inspection that every filing cabinet, every desk drawer, all my school and business papers had been dumped over the floor. As I raced into the darkness, I started slipping as my feet skidded on the papery surface. I would have surely fallen except for the arms that reached out and pulled me forward.

This couldn't be my pursuer from the attic, I recall reasoning through my confusion. *He'd be behind me.*

Why didn't I scream? Because familiar arms were cradling me momentarily; because his familiar voice at my ear quickly whispered, "It's Michael."

Had he actually said his full name, Nick Michaels? At that moment it was what I assumed he had said, and in my confusion I figured that I'd heard only Michael.

In any case, even though I could not make him out plainly in the dark, and even though when he released me to hold me by the shoulders at arms' length, I still could not make out any discernible features, there was no question in my mind about who he was.

"Now," he whispered at me, "do exactly as I say. No matter what happens, don't move from here. Don't make a sound. Promise!"

I kept staring at the dark form in front of me and didn't respond.

He shook me slightly. "Promise!" he hissed louder.

I nodded my head and he let me go. It was when he had turned toward the lighted hallway door that I saw why his features had been obscured. I was staring at the Disco King in all his beard and long hair and loose clothing!

I had no time to respond with either a gasp or a comment because, in despair, I watched as a second figure suddenly appeared at the doorway directly in Nick's path.

I shrank down even further into the room and, crouching low on the floor, inched my back up against the brown studio divan. There I waited for the ultimate skirmish to erupt.

"Oh, it's you, Nick!" I heard the second form exclaim.

"Percy! God, man, they had you dead, man!" It was Nick's voice but not his usual manner of speaking.

And then the phone started ringing. I tried to listen to the men's conversation over the high-pitched clanging of its bell only inches from me on the desk, but the two figures moved off, and I didn't catch any more of their exchange. I huddled there on the floor willing the phone to be still. The notion of answering it never crossed my mind. I kept trying to fight the urgent impulse to run, to get out of the house, but the feeling was countered by my instinct to hide, to do as Nick had instructed.

But who was Nick? Who was the intruder, Percy?

Percy was not a common name. What Nick had said about his being dead could only mean that he was Percy Hapinsky. But how did Nick know Percy? And why were they both in my house uninvited? Hell, how had they gotten in?

Conversation I had heard at the boarded-up houses began to replay in my mind, as if in answer to my questions, but the phone and my fear kept distracting any coherent thoughts.

Then the ringing suddenly stopped and I wondered who could have been calling at what must now be after four A.M.

What if it had been Jana?

I was seized then by the agonizing fear that my daughter, across the court, had gotten up to go to the bathroom, looked over here and seen the house all lighted up, and dialed me to find out if everything was all right. Then the obvious next step in my sequential reasoning: having received no answer to over a dozen rings, she would take it upon herself to come home and check on me!

I strained to hear voices or footsteps to alert me to where the men were. All I could hear were muffled tones so indistinct that they droned meaninglessly, but I knew they came from the direction of Franny's room. If Jana were on her way here, I had to stop her. That meant I would have to be prepared to dash past Franny's door, through the hall, and down the stairs so fast that the men would not have time to react or catch up with me, at least until I was outside the house and could scream for help. If possible, maybe Jana could get back to the Burgesses' and call the police. Certainly, the promise I had made to Nick melted in view of the fact that Jana might be walking into danger.

Without a sound, I pressed my elbows into the roughness of the couch behind me, and with my feet braced in front, rose awkwardly but noiselessly to a standing position.

I crept to the door, glad to hear the voices louder now, so I could definitely place them in Franny's room to my left.

I didn't wait any longer. Flinging myself forward, I used the hallway walls to push myself even faster toward the stairs, and reaching them, hurled myself down, sliding dangerously off many steps as I grasped the railing to keep from falling altogether. As I slid past the bottom stair and landed on my feet on the foyer floor, I was not surprised to hear the doorbell ring.

In a panic to head off Jana before the men upstairs could stop me, I thrust the deadbolt back and pulled the door open. I had intended to burst outside and close the door behind me, but in my haste to do that, I ran straight into not Jana, but Happy.

"Whoa, Kiddo," he said, and I was stunned when he roughly shoved me back against the foyer wall and stepped quickly inside, slamming the door and bolting it securely behind him.

I saw the gun in the second he turned from fastening the lock. He had been holding it all along.

"I didn't really want to do it this way, Kiddo," he said to my shocked expression, "but it's the only way."

"Happy, what are you doing? I can't believe you'd ever use that thing!" My trembling voice belied the conviction of my words.

"Afraid so, Kiddo," he said, pointing the weapon directly at me, then waving it toward the center of the foyer to indicate for me to move out of his way and away from the door. "This gun has killed family; guess it won't stop at neighbors, either," he muttered as I obeyed his directions and moved to the center of the hall opposite the archway into the living room.

I heard the scuffle of feet, muted by the floor and carpeting just above my head. I knew by the look on Happy's face that he had heard it, too.

"Who's up there?" he growled, and the sinister look on his face was one I would never have suspected Happy could have produced. It twisted his features into an evil mask that filled me with terror. Involuntarily, I began to shrink back from him, but the gun stabbed at the air between us as he silently commanded me to stay still.

"Who's up there?" he growled again.

"It's only me, Pops," a voice replied from somewhere above our heads. I couldn't tell if Percy was still on the second floor or if he was halfway down the stairs, hidden just behind the partition where the wrought-iron railing met the wall.

Happy's evil mask disintegrated in an instant, and a new expression— which I interpreted as utter disbelief—replaced it. Forgetting about me, he spun around and confronted an empty stairway.

"What's the matter, Pops? You look like you've seen a ghost." The tone was taunting and close. I was sure Percy had to be just beyond the wall in the semidarkness of the stairs.

Happy raised his gun toward the voice!

"Uh-uh, Pops. Can't kill me twice. Come up and we'll talk. I'll cut you a deal. That's a lot more than you did for me."

Happy kept the gun raised, but something in his demeanor suggested that he was becoming confused, uncertain. His entire body was frozen in a grotesque position, his legs parted, knees slightly bent, his right arm straight up in the air with the gun perched in his curled fingers. His other arm was bent uselessly in an arc at his left side. He looked like a petrified Roadrunner.

Careful not to move my body and draw Happy's attention back to me, I turned my head to assess my chances of fleeing from where I stood at the edge of the foyer. If I ran to my left and into the kitchen, Happy would be able to shoot me before I disappeared around the corner. There was no way I could get to the door and unbolt it and get out of the house without getting hit, either. As I looked in back of my right shoulder to study an escape route through the living room, I saw that the room was awash in blue lights.

I remember wondering if I should be relieved or even more fearful. With the police approaching from outside, and Percy above, Happy was trapped. But I was in the middle! If Happy panicked, I was standing out like a sore thumb.

And Nick! What was his part in all this? Percy had not let on that he was not alone up there. Were the two of them in cahoots? Cahoots about what, for God's sake?

"What will it be, Pops?" Percy pushed. "Look, I'm tired; come up so we can talk. You'll never find the stuff without me."

I looked behind me toward the blue living room.

"You must think I was born yesterday," came Happy's reply. I'm supposed to trust you after what you and your folks pulled on me?"

"I'll show you where I stashed everything. My drowning," Percy snorted, "took a lot out of me, so I need help to get at it. You give me a hand, and I'll cut you in."

As the two men were talking, I had inched my way along the wall until I was positioned at the inside of the archway where I could duck behind the living room partition.

Happy must have been considering Percy's offer because he glanced at me then with an expression that said, "What do I do with Kiddo if I go to help Percy?" I wasn't sure if he realized I had managed to move to a new position or not, but he did a double-take into the living room area, where even more lights were flashing now.

"The police," I said unnecessarily. I looked away from Happy's wild expression and concentrated on his gun. If time ever actually stands still, it stood still at that moment—for me, anyway. I could sense the turmoil of decision-making on Happy's part, and for an instant he forgot about the gun, for I saw it begin to lower almost imperceptibly as his attention was diverted to the front of the house and then back to me.

"They'll be in riot formation about now," I said in as calm a tone as I could muster.

"Piss on 'em," Happy said, but his focus had been off of the stairs for too many seconds. In his momentary distraction, a shot came from somewhere on the stairs, and caught Happy in his right hand. His gun went flying.

Percy went flying also. He never touched a step as Nick, holding him by the back of his shirt collar, forced him down the staircase. I had time to notice a pistol in Nick's right hand before I watched Percy strike the abutting wall head first at the edge of the lower stair.

Happy, his right hand covered in blood, was bent over trying to retrieve the gun with his good hand and took all of Percy's weight when his grandson landed on him. The two men lay in a heap at the foot of the stairway.

Nick's foot landed on top of Percy, pinning both grandson and grandfather to the floor.

Too stunned to move for cover (which I had planned to do if things got violent) I had managed to kick the gun farther away from Happy. Now I picked it up.

Nick looked over at me. "Are you okay?" he asked.

I nodded and handed him the gun.

"Let them in," he instructed, gesturing with his head toward the door, and it was only then that I became aware of frenzied pounding and calls of "Open up! Police!"

I stepped around the two men at the bottom of the stairs. I saw Nick's foot press with greater force into their backs when Happy attempted to move an arm out into my path.

I released the bolt and turned the doorknob.

The sergeant was on the other side of the screen, his gun raised and pointed at me.

From somewhere at the back of the house came the explosive sound of glass breaking. I remember worrying that the sergeant was about to shoot me and that the riot squad had just pulverized my sliding glass door. Not necessarily in that order.

"The screen's unlocked," I told the sergeant and stepped back.

The sergeant didn't move. "What seems to be the trouble?" he asked me.

"What the hell is keeping him?" Nick growled from the stairs. "Tell him to get in here!" From where he was, Nick could not see the sergeant standing motionless on the steps, and the sergeant could not see Nick or the two men he hovered over because the opened door blocked his view.

"What's going down here?" the sergeant asked in a louder voice. Nick must have heard him then because he put the gun he was holding in his left hand down on a step behind him and dug into the back pocket of his tattered jeans, pulling out a piece of plastic.

"Show him this and tell him to get the hell in here. I could use some help," he muttered to me.

I held up the piece of plastic as I advanced toward the screen and kept an eye on the sergeant's gun.

"That you, Mike?" the sergeant yelled as he gingerly, I thought, opened the door.

"O'Leary?" Nick yelled back. "Get me two pairs of cuffs and give me a hand, for God's sake!"

Still pointing the gun at me, O'Leary entered the hall. When he saw the two men in a pile under Nick's foot, he cursed and shifted the direction of the weapon he was holding away from me and onto the two men.

"I've got 'em covered, O'Leary," Nick scoffed, "just give me some handcuffs."

The sergeant lunged toward the door and began to bark out orders. "Get in here!" he commanded as if it were the officers who were holding up the operation. "Gimme those," he ordered the first two men who came through the door, referring to the handcuffs at their belts.

I escaped from the gathering of police in my foyer. I'd already witnessed that scene too many times before. I went into the dining room to look at my glass slider. It was in one piece, but all of the side window, top and bottom, had been smashed. I couldn't figure out why, since it had been open all night for air. Two officers were just crawling in through the casement.

I sank into the chair at the table. The same one I had been in the evening before—before I'd started to follow Nick and the blonde woman.

Nick. The sergeant had called him Mike. He was evidently a cop. Wonderful! He could have saved me all the worry and aggravation by telling me that simple fact at the start. Why hadn't he?

I buried my face in my hands, too tired to care. It was then that I started shaking. I just couldn't stop. I felt suddenly cold and weak and incapable of controlling the massive tremors that wracked my body. Nick came around the corner then, took one look at me, and, kneeling down beside my chair, took me into his arms.

"It's a normal reaction," he said. "Just go with it for a minute. Then you need to get some sleep."

"I need to get some answers," I said against a phony beard that was irritating my nose. My voice was shaking as uncontrollably as my body, and that made me feel like a fool, but I kept talking.

"Who the hell are you?" I quaked.

"My name is Mike Nichols," he said in an easy tone that was calculated, I figured, to calm me down.

"Mike Nichols," I repeated. "Nick Michaels! Cute! Clever! I suppose you're what's called an undercover cop."

"That's right," same even, annoying tone.

"And what the hell are you undercovering in my house? Or is that classified information or something?"

I don't know what was bothering me most, his beard scratching my nose, his placating tone of voice, or his breath, warm against my ear.

"Mom!" I heard my daughter's voice full of apprehension and disbelief. "What happened? Are you hurt?"

I pulled my face out of Nick's beard, and Nick stood up and stepped away from me. I held out my arms toward Jana. "I'm okay," and I managed a remote smile before I hugged her.

"I saw all the police lights when I got up to go to the bathroom," she said, hugging me tightly around the neck. "I thought you'd been hurt or. . . something." Her voice trailed off weakly as she contemplated whatever fears had been in her mind.

Then I felt her decidedly stiffen, and she stopped talking in a regular voice. "Mom," she whispered, "the guy behind me. . .the one who was hugging you when I came in. . .isn't that. . .?"

". . .the Disco King," I finished for her.

Jana dropped her arms from around my neck and pulled back to gaze at her heartthrob. He was now standing just beyond the archway in the living room talking to Sergeant O'Leary.

"Why were you two hugging?" Jana asked, looking at me with raised eyebrows.

"He's an undercover cop," I said simply, ignoring the suspicious look and its implications. "He was consoling me. If it hadn't been for him, I'd be dead."

My words startled me. Of course, they were true. Had he not been here, there was no telling what Happy or Percy would have done. "He saved my life," I said again, as if I needed to reinforce that reality for myself.

"Janet!" Joey's voice in the front hall interrupted Jana's next question.

"I'm in here, Joey."

"Thank God!" was all he said as he rounded the corner of the dining room and saw that I was all in one piece. He gave me a hug and over his shoulder, my eyes met Nick's watching the reunion from the next room.

Joey stood back and gave me a sweeping examination. "You look ghastly," he declared.

I ignored his flattery and looked past him to where Nick had been standing. He was gone. Pointlessly, I tried to recall the name of the country where a person whose life is saved belongs to her rescuer.

"Janet!" Franny rushed into the dining room and halted just in front of me. "Are you all right?" she asked, and I could tell by her voice and her face that she was truly anguished.

I nodded and was ashamed to feel tears welling up in my eyes.

"Did Nick leave?" I don't know where that question came from. I hadn't realized I was going to ask it.

"He went down to the station; paperwork, that sort of thing. I was working with him, you know," she added.

"I just figured that out," I said. "Why didn't you let me in on what was going on?"

"They wouldn't let me. They thought you might be involved.

I knew you weren't, but I didn't have anything to say about it. They granted me immunity if I cooperated."

"Immunity!" I gasped. "You mean—?"

"My husband and I were part of the Hapinsky ring for a long time. I wanted out, but in order to *get* out, I needed help. The police offered me protection in return for my assistance in gathering evidence against the entire group. That's when I spilled the beans about my husband's and my involvement. I had begged Larry to get out with me, of course, but he refused. He was arrested immediately.

"The police suspected that drugs were being stashed in this house, and convinced me to move in here where they could keep an eye on me, and I could better help them. So I made up the story about needing a temporary place to stay."

"But why were drugs here? And how did they get here, for God's sake?"

"It was Percy who was getting in through the window of the room that had been his bedroom when he and his parents lived in the house. He'd climb up the tiered chimney and in the bedroom window just as he had done as a teenager when he wanted to sneak out late and come in undetected. The police figure he was holding back some of the drugs and building up his own stash in the attic. That may be why Happy tried to kill him. It may be the key to what happened to Percy's parents, as well. They haven't been seen since the sale of the house."

"Nice family," muttered Joey, who had been pacing the floor and listening silently. "Thank God I called the police," he added.

Both Franny and I spoke together then. "*You* called the police?"

"I couldn't sleep all night after I left here." Joey groaned and slumped into a chair beside me at the table. "It must have been about three-thirty when I threw on a bathrobe and got into the car. Imagine me, 'Natty Ned,' driving around town in a bathrobe! Anyway, I drove over here and what do I see but every light in the house on!

"Now I'm in a real panic. Should I stop and try to get in; ring the bell; bang on the door? I decided to go home and call first. I figured maybe Janet just had all the lights on because she's less jittery that way. So I called. I let the phone ring at least a dozen times. I figured no one could sleep through that many rings! So I hung up and paced a few more minutes, trying to decide what to do next, and finally I decided to call the police. I reminded them of the earlier break-in and told them that things didn't look right when I drove by the house; could they please take a look."

"Thanks, Joey," I said. "At the time the phone was ringing, Nick was in Franny's room—Percy's old room—with Percy, and I was hiding out in the den."

I didn't mention that my reason for opening the door to Happy was my fear that the caller had been Jana, and I'd wanted to warn her. Why make Joey feel guilty about bringing on what turned out to be the right ending? "All's well that ends well," I concluded, smiling faintly.

"Mom," Jana said from across the room, where she'd been taking this all in, "why don't you get some sleep now? Franny's here, and she and I can get rid of the rest of the police department and make sure you're not disturbed for a while."

I looked at the clock over the hutch: five-thirty. Sun was beginning to brighten the back decks behind me. I was absolutely exhausted, but I wasn't ready to give in. "I'm too wound," I said. "Besides, do you know how cluttered my bedroom is? I can't relax in all that mess."

Franny took over then. "Jana," she directed, "go get Terrance out of the car and put him in the dog run; then go see if Laurie will help you start work on Mom's room. I'll be right up to help as soon as I get your mother some Dubonnet. A few sips of that and she'll be out like a light."

Jana took off on her mission, and I stared at Franny. "Terrance?" I said. I was suddenly elated.

"Now, Janet, don't get upset," Franny cautioned, misunderstanding my reaction. "I won't let him in the house again, I promise."

"Terrance?" I said again. "He's all right? You found him?"

"He wasn't lost this time. I knew the police were hiding him at the boarded-up houses until this case was cracked. Terrance screwed up a couple of Percy's attempts to gain access to the upstairs. By staying out late, I made sure I didn't get in Percy's way, but the detectives didn't like Terrance. They grabbed him the first time, when he chased Percy out of the house through the cellar door. I had no idea they had done that or that the boarded-up houses were government property and a base for the drug team. They clued me in fast after my rampage against that door, but shortly after my one-woman attack on the place, Terrance escaped. It was Mike Nichols who made it clear that, should Terrance come home, the dog was not part of the surveillance team and would be permanently removed."

The memory of Franny in heated discussion with my neighbor in the shadow of his driveway the night that Terrance returned replayed in my mind.

I was still thinking about it when Franny brought me a glass of Dubonnet on the rocks. I took a delicious sip and realized suddenly how hungry I was.

"Franny," I said, "there's leftover potato salad and fried chicken in the refrigerator."

I had to say no more.

Once she had placed two heaping plates of food in front of us, I was anxious to continue our talk. We were finally alone. The police had left a half hour before after boarding up the broken window, and Joey had drunk a quick cup of coffee and hurried home to shower and change before reporting to work. The girls had returned and were chatting in animated voices as they worked on tidying my room. They had looked at us in horror when we'd offered to share some of our unorthodox breakfast with them.

"We'll hit you up for some Egg McMuffins later," Jana had laughed.

Life had begun to tumble back into some semblance of normalcy already, it seemed.

"Franny," I managed to say through a mouthful of potato salad, "two nights ago when Terrance disappeared a second time, was that Percy's shadow I saw in the upstairs hall?"

"It wasn't any of the detectives that night," Franny answered. "It must have been Percy. Mike, as you know, was in the bushes, and two other guys were on lookout behind the house as they usually were each night in anticipation of a visit by Percy to the bedroom. Mike had to stop you from calling for help so Percy could get away. He wasn't ready to make an arrest. He needed to be sure he had all the culprits first. Then Terrance ran out of the house again that night, and one of our guys grabbed him. This time I was prepared for his disappearance."

Franny put her fork down and leaned forward. "Will you ever forgive me for this whole charade?" she asked, and I knew she was truly worried that I would not. "I'm embarrassed about being involved in the drug scene to begin with, but I regret even more getting you involved in an effort to save my ass. I didn't think you'd be in any danger. We just hadn't counted on Happy being the ringleader. I had no idea he was involved in the operation at all. I had dealt only with Percy and his parents. Those were the three we were waiting to nab."

I took a slow sip of my wine and set it down solemnly. "Franny," I said, "I do forgive you. And better than that, I even love your dog."

Franny gave me a broad smile. As we resumed eating, she chatted and chuckled like the old Franny I had been missing lately.

I took another long sip of Dubonnet and a deep breath, and plunged into a new matter. "Did Nick think I was guilty of being an accomplice to this operation?" I asked, trying to make my question sound as matter-of-fact as my others had been.

"Mike, you mean? He never thought you were involved," she answered, "but some of the others weren't so sure. So we had to operate as though you were. There's no worry now that it's over. It's obvious that you had no knowledge of any of this."

I nodded numbly and took another long breath. "Was Dale involved? I remember him appearing so quickly after my accident with Nick's car."

"Dale was one of the contacts with the regular force. When you hit Mike's car, Mike sent him around to make sure you and the Burgesses didn't get suspicious or cause any trouble for him. . Do you remember hearing that wailing truck and the music from Percy's stereo just before you hit Mike?"

I nodded.

"The music was always the signal that Percy was ready to trade with the dealers in the truck, who would signal back. So Mike had to get in position to observe the transfer. That was why he was in such a hurry."

I was beginning to feel fuzzy-headed, and suspected that my nose could be in the potato salad any minute now. I might as well ask all my questions while I was still conscious.

"Does Nick have a wife or a girlfriend?"

Franny glanced up at me quickly, but didn't so much as blink. "He's divorced. I know of no girlfriend," she added without comment.

"Franny, you're a woman of the world. If you had a crush on a guy, would you try to let him know it?"

I thought I saw the corners of her mouth twitch. "You mean if I had the hots for a guy, would I come on to him?"

"I guess that's what I mean," I said, raising my glass shakily to my lips.

Franny took the glass from my hand and helped me out of my chair.

I vaguely remember her putting me to bed. I think Jana came in and gave me a kiss, and I remember Franny closing the shades and curtains against the morning sun.

I fell into a long and wonderfully deep sleep full of actively changing colors and shapes and intriguing plots. I woke up once in the early evening, long enough to have a drink of water and learn that Mike Nichols had stopped by to inquire about how I was.

Or was that part of one of my dreams? I'm not sure. Without finishing a complete glass of liquid, I lay back down in exhaustion and dropped off to sleep for the rest of the night.

CHAPTER 15

That was a week ago.
Since then, my life has shifted quickly back to the normal patterns.

I get up at five and walk every morning. An hour later, I go back to the house and make a pot of coffee and spend the next hour on the front steps watching the Peddington lawn grow greener and wondering if my own lawn will ever begin to flourish.

Mrs. Murphy still sets bowls of goodies outside her door about seven every morning, and I wave to Martha when she comes out to feed the birds her breakfast leavings.

The only thing to have changed, really, is that Happy no longer jogs by with a "Good morning, Kiddo" and a wave. Happy's house is deserted, and I do not know what has happened to poor Sarah. Percy and his grandfather will serve a great deal of jail time from what Dale tells me when he stops by in the cruiser to chat, and Happy may serve the rest of his life if it is ever proved that Percy's parents were murdered by his hand.

I have not seen Mike Nichols since the morning he rescued me from the Hapinskys. Franny says he is busy making new plans for his career. His cover was blown the morning he pulled the gun on Percy and Happy, but he has had several offers from various police forces around the country and from government agencies, as well.

I try not to think about him, but he's constantly on my mind. I tell myself that if I never see him again, it will help me forget the frightening episode more quickly.

Jana can't believe someone so old turned out to be the Disco

King. "He looked so ancient once he was out of the car," she kept saying over and over for days afterward.

"You ought to see him out of his beard," Franny told her. "Your Mom thinks he's really cool without the beard!"

"Do you, Mom?" Jana had asked as I shot Franny a dirty look.

"You know, Jana," Franny had said as she totally ignored me, "one of these days, your mother will start dating. Maybe very soon."

"Mom isn't interested in men," Jana had told her. "She's just like me. Independent."

Franny kidded Jana a lot about that remark from then on.

Today marks a week since the electric outage and the Hapinsky arrests. I was up this morning at five and had walked six miles when I returned and found Franny busy at her car with a bunch of boxes.

"Time to go," she announced glibly as I came across Grayson Street and asked what she was up to. "You don't have to move out all in one day, do you?" I protested. "We've just begun to enjoy each other's company again."

"I never really needed a place to stay," she reminded me. "Terrance needs his own backyard, and I need my own space. Besides, I have a feeling that three's a crowd."

I looked at her with a puzzled expression.

"Mike Nichols came home last night," she said.

"How do you know?" I asked. Franny nodded toward the corner. I realized then that familiar rock music was echoing louder and louder from that direction. In surprise, I watched as the equally familiar, paint-stripped convertible rounded the corner.

"What's he doing?" I asked Franny. "He can't be back in that disguise around here."

"Look again," she laughed. The car slowed and turned into the court. The driver, truly a teenager, boasted a full head of long hair, but no beard.

"Mike's son," Franny explained. "That's where he was this week. In New York, picking Bobby up to spend the summer. Guess Bobby likes the wheels, and Mike has no more use for them."

From the upstairs window, a voice, groggy from sleep, paged

me. "Mom," Jana croaked, "how come he's back to the undercover stuff again? Another case?"

"I'll tell you later," I tried to whisper. After all, it was early in the morning, and between rock music and Jana's window broadcast, the neighborhood probably thought it was in for another siege.

"How old is Bobby?" I asked Franny, rather dreading the answer.

"Just turned seventeen, I think," came the answer I was dreading.

I left Franny to wrestle with the boxes and suitcases and grabbed a quick shower. While I slid into a fresh shorts-and-halter set and blew my hair dry, I heard voices from downstairs. Franny's voice. And a man's!

I dabbed on some mascara and lipstick, and with my heart pumping like a schoolgirl's, descended the stairs.

He and Franny were sitting at the dining room table having coffee. He looked up to meet my eyes when I entered.

The moment I stepped into the doorway, Franny stood up and declared she had oodles of packing still to do—and she left. I mean, she just disappeared.

Mike looked rested and tanned and absolutely gorgeous! He also looked amused. If Franny's exit was delighting him, it was thoroughly embarrassing me. I had everything to do to keep myself focused on calming my beating heart and wiping off what I imagined to be an insipid, adolescent, love-starved expression all over my face.

"Why don't we take some coffee onto the deck," I said too stiffly.

"Good idea," Mike nodded, rising out of his chair, and in dismay, I realized he was following me into the kitchen while I poured a cup of coffee for myself. The moment the two of us were at the coffee pot, the room was overpowered by Mike Nichols's presence.

"Here," his voice near my ear said, "do this again," and his bare arm brushed mine ever so lightly as he passed his cup in front of me to be refilled.

I managed not to spill a drop or tremble when I poured, but I cannot remember when I've felt so miserable. Or so joyful.

We took our cups out onto the deck and sat at the picnic table, the same table where I'd sat dozens of times watching him come and go and wondering who he was and what his life was like.

Mike Nichols didn't waste time. Once we were seated opposite each other, he put his cup down and leaned forward far enough to take both my hands in his.

"I want the air cleared from the start," he said, looking me right in the eyes and holding my gaze. "First, I never believed you were part of this operation; not ever! Since the first day I moved in there," he nodded across the court toward his green house, "and you came out of this slider wearing that bright orange swimsuit, I knew you couldn't be part of anything ugly."

"I could have sworn you never noticed me," I said, suddenly forgetting to be nervous.

"Tricks of the trade," Mike laughed. "I'm a good cop. No one knows when she's under surveillance. I noticed!" he finished with a serious and penetrating expression in his eyes that made me look away because I could feel the color climbing into my face.

"I can sense a tension between us this morning, and I don't blame you for feeling leery, but you've got to believe that I don't usually grab women or force myself on them. Not even beautiful ones," he added pointedly.

I felt myself blushing more. He gave my hands a light squeeze and let them go. "I apologize for all of my behavior," he said, sitting back and taking his coffee cup up to his lips for a sip. "Grabbing you like that in the middle of the night! Twice!" Mike shook his head and avoided my eyes as he set the cup back down. "The first time, I worried you'd blow the whistle on Percy; the second time, under the streetlight, that my cover would be blown. Had we not been standing there like that, though, I might not have tied Happy in so quickly, so I thank you for that—and for helping us grab the damn dog that second time, of course."

"You sound like you didn't like Terrance," I snickered, glad for a humorous detour in the conversation.

Mike's eyes returned to my face with a hint of mischief

in them. "Terrance didn't like me," he said. "I was the one who trapped him in the cellar the first time we captured him. That's why he came at me the day you hit my car."

The incident replayed itself in my mind and reminded me to mention that I knew that Dale had been involved in the investigation.

Mike nodded. "He and Sergeant O'Leary were my only contacts on the local force. O'Leary was scary, totally inept, but he had to know what I was doing. Dale is a great cop. I'm sure he'll get the permanent promotion that he wants, and it will be because of his role in this assignment."

We sat silently for several seconds. He took another sip of his coffee and set his cup down. "I wish I could erase it all and start with 'Would you like to go to dinner tonight?'" he said, looking straight into my eyes.

"I would love to go out to dinner tonight," I heard myself say, and we both laughed and eased a bit of the discomfort we had been feeling.

Sometime soon, I thought to myself as I walked him to the front door, *I'll confess to you that some of the tension you felt between us today was caused by your damn brown eyes and cologne wafting too closely around my head, and your opened shirt, all of which were making me crazy. Sometime soon, perhaps I'll even tell you how much I want us to retrace out steps back to that lamppost and throw rocks through its light and get back into our embrace and move on from there.*

"Did you only begin to suspect Happy that night under the streetlight?" I asked instead, when we'd reached the front door.

"The music that was playing when the electricity came back on was always the signal between Percy and his gang. But Percy was supposed to be dead by the time the electricity went off. So I knew that either Percy was alive, or Happy was in on the drug trafficking in some way. As it turned out, both scenarios were true," he shrugged. "We're working on the distinct possibility that Happy knocked off his own son and daughter-in-law because they were undercutting his shipments with Percy."

"And Happy was in my house looking for Percy's stuff?" I asked as Mike and I lingered in the foyer.

"With Percy gone, he figured he'd just come in and take it back. Obviously, he focused on the main floors. He never figured on the attic the first time, but he was clearly coming back for another look."

"And I let him in. Blew your cover," I said by way of an apology.

"Thankfully, Percy trusted me and hated his father, so he was willing to engage him in conversation while I got a bead on him without risking your safety. As for losing my cover, it was time. I'm too old for this game. Time to move on."

"Tell me how Percy turned up alive. I saw how stunned Happy was when he heard his voice. I can believe he thought he'd killed him."

"I think so, too," Mike nodded. "Percy is, as they say, singing like a bird, and we are learning a great deal. Evidently, Happy followed his grandson and a group of his friends to Great Lake and waited until Percy was separated from them. Then he whacked him over the head. While Percy lay unconscious, Happy held his head under water long enough, he thought, for the kid to drown, but minutes after Happy left, Percy came to and took off fast to avoid whoever had attacked him. He was pretty sure it was his grandfather because by that time, he had real fears about what had happened to his parents. In the meantime, when the rest of the group couldn't find Percy, they called the police thinking he had drowned while they were diving and horsing around in the water. I guess they had been doing drugs and drinking a lot since they'd arrived that morning."

Jana interrupted us as she raced down the stairs with a cryptic announcement that she was off to Laurie's. She had apparently been up for some time because her hair was freshly done, and there was, on closer inspection, a hint of makeup.

"Is that makeup?" I asked.

"Where?" She was giving me the hand on the extended hip routine and the "you've got me" smile that always managed to creep across her face like it had a life of its own when she was guilty.

"It's only ten-thirty," I said, deciding not to take on the issue of mascara just now. "Is Laurie even up yet?"

"We've been on the phone for hours," she sighed with impatience. "There's a new boy in the neighborhood."

Then she noticed Mike was chuckling.

"My son, Bobby," he said. "Come on, I'll introduce you."

"Really, Mr. Nichols?" My daughter was beaming with delight. "Wait till I tell Laurie this!" And she would have dashed out the door then, except Franny, carrying a suitcase, cut off her exit as she made the last pass to her loaded car.

As Jana held the door open for her, I heard Franny mumble something about a short-lived independence, and saw my daughter blush.

I was laughing to myself as I followed everyone out onto the steps.

"Seven?" Mike mouthed back over his shoulder to me with a wink as he hurried to catch up with Jana.

I nodded and watched in amusement as my daughter passed Franny at her car. Jana gave her the famous Dicky Dunlap salute in an effort, I surmised, to ward off further editorial comment. At that point, Mike caught up to her, and by the time they had reached the corner, Jana was chattering away to a bemused-looking Mike Nichols.

I went out to the curb to assist Franny just as Terrance came dashing out from around the house dragging his chain like Marley's ghost. The first shrub by the steps and then my maple took a direct hit before he caught up to Franny and started to jump all over her and then me.

"I'm going to miss you, Franny," I said. "And your little dog, too," I added in my best Wicked Witch of the West voice.

After all that had happened—or perhaps I should say, *because* of all that had happened—I felt a huge lump begin to form in my throat.

"I won't be a stranger," she said, giving me a hug. "Besides," she added, "when you get ready to break every streetlight on the block, I want to be a witness to it."

Stunned, I looked at her, my mouth hanging open.

"I told you I was psychic," she shrugged. When my mouth failed to close, she added, "Okay, truth be told, you do tend to talk in your sleep after a Dubonnet."

The old-age home was watching, I'm sure, as the two of us laughed and cried our good-byes, like idiots, at the curb.

Also by JANE HARVEY MEADE

Remembering Peter
Glimpses
Love Amidst Abuse

Coming in 2012
The Season in Between
and
A Single Woman (The Anatomy of a Divorce)

For more information about any of the above books,
log onto my website:
www.janeharveymeade.com